"What about your underthings?"

Michael asked. "You can't keep them on. They'll be wet and cold. Look at you, you're shivering already."

Pema clutched her towel under her chin as she reached underneath with both hands to unclasp her bra.

Michael grinned. "Surely you're not shy. A woman of nature like you? Don't you know the human body is merely another life form?"

She glared at him.

"Pema," he said, "your body is beautiful, and I meant what I said. It's natural—everyone has a body. But if you want, I'll turn around."

Pema thought for a moment. She probably looked ridiculous trying to hide behind a scrap of terry. Michael was right. Her body was a part of her, part of the natural environment. She lifted her chin.

Michael forced his face to remain expressionless, his breathing to stay steady. After his speech about bodies being simply natural, he could hardly start to pant over hers.

But he wished he could.

Dear Reader,

At Silhouette Romance we're starting the New Year off right! This month we're proud to present *Donavan*, the ninth wonderful book in Diana Palmer's enormously popular LONG, TALL TEXANS series. *The Taming of the Teen* is a delightful sequel to Marie Ferrarella's *Man Trouble*—and Marie promises that Angelo's story is coming soon. Maggi Charles returns with the tantalizing *Keep It Private* and Jody McCrae makes her debut with the charming *Lake of Dreams*. Pepper Adams's *That Old Black Magic* casts a spell of love in the Louisiana bayou—but watch out for Crevi the crocodile!

Of course, no lineup in 1992 would be complete without our special WRITTEN IN THE STARS selection. This month we're featuring the courtly Capricorn man in Joan Smith's *For Richer, for Poorer*.

Throughout the year we'll be publishing stories of love by all of your favorite Silhouette Romance authors—Diana Palmer, Brittany Young, Annette Broadrick, Suzanne Carey and many, many more. The Silhouette Romance authors and editors love to hear from readers, and we'd love to hear from *you!*

Happy New Year... and happy reading!

Valerie Susan Hayward
Senior Editor

JODY McCRAE

Lake of Dreams

Silhouette Romance

Published by Silhouette Books New York

America's Publisher of Contemporary Romance

For the Saskatoon Romance Writers—
one for all and all for one

SILHOUETTE BOOKS
300 E. 42nd St., New York, N.Y. 10017

LAKE OF DREAMS

Copyright © 1992 by Judy McCrosky

All rights reserved. Except for use in any review, the reproduction or utilization of this work in whole or in part in any form by any electronic, mechanical or other means, now known or hereafter invented, including xerography, photocopying and recording, or in any information storage or retrieval system, is forbidden without the permission of the publisher, Silhouette Books, 300 E. 42nd St., New York, N.Y. 10017

ISBN: 0-373-08841-8

First Silhouette Books printing January 1992

All the characters in this book have no existence outside the imagination of the author and have no relation whatsoever to anyone bearing the same name or names. They are not even distantly inspired by any individual known or unknown to the author, and all incidents are pure invention.

®: Trademark used under license and registered in the United States Patent and Trademark Office and in other countries.

Printed in the U.S.A.

JODY McCRAE

was born in Aberdeen, Scotland, but lived there only ten days before moving to California. She's often wished she could have stayed long enough to pick up a sexy Scottish accent!

Jody and her husband live in Saskatchewan with their two children. One of their favorite family activities is canoeing through the rugged beauty of the Canadian Shield, and Jody is pleased to have translated this love into her first book.

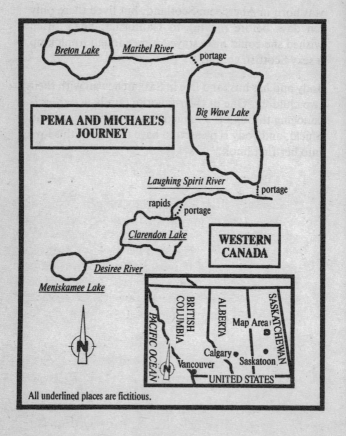

Chapter One

Pema pressed a little harder on the accelerator as she sped along the narrow highway that ran through fields of young wheat. As she glanced up at the cloudless sky, her red hair tumbled away from her face and cascaded down her back. A smile curved her lips, a smile that felt as wide as the fields that stretched to either side of her. It was maybe reckless to drive so fast, but the road was straight, dry and deserted, and she felt so good she just had to fly.

It was a glorious June day and freedom was near. Soon, only days from now, she would be gone, gliding along quiet streams, paddling across lakes, on her way to Meniskamee.

Meniskamee. Her lake. And Grandfather's, too, of course. He would be there, waiting for her. Pema wrinkled her nose, knowing that her friends sometimes worried about her when she spoke of her grandfather like this. He had passed away a year ago. But Pema knew that he had never really left her. He was there, in her spirit, and nowhere did she feel closer to him than at the lake where the two of them had spent so much time together.

Her earliest memory was of Meniskamee. She had been helping Grandfather build his cabin, and she remembered stirring the cement, pushing a big stick around and around through the thick gray muck, her little hands gripping the wood between his large ones. Soon she would be there again. One more exam to give tomorrow, and school was over for the year. The summer lay before her, filled with light glinting off water and night skies warm with stars. A summer to canoe through.

But first she needed to find out why her brothers had called her for a family council. Three of her brothers lived on the farm, which lay thirty miles outside Saskatoon, deep in the Saskatchewan wheat country. She saw her brother John more often, since he lived, as she did, in the city. He worked as a construction site carpenter, and helped on the farm whenever he could. But all five of them shared joint responsibility and ownership of the farm, and when decisions needed to be made, as she suspected was the case today, the five of them took council together.

She turned onto the dirt road that led to the farm, and soon her car tires were crunching on the gravel drive that made a loop in front of the Robinson farmhouse. Getting out, she looked up and saw three of her brothers coming out to greet her.

"Hi, guys," she cried. Running up, she gave her oldest brother, Peter, a hug. "It's been ages since I've seen you. Why, it must be all of two weeks!"

LAKE OF DREAMS

Peter smiled and hugged his sister. George and James, the twins, came forward for their hugs. Nondemonstrative among themselves, the brothers had lavished all the love and affection in their hearts on their young sister. Fifteen years younger than Peter, and twelve and ten years younger than the others, Pema had been raised by her brothers. Their mother had died at her birth, and their father only a few years later.

"So, what's up?" Pema went into the house. The door led to a large, sunny kitchen, which was filled with the scent of fresh coffee. Pine cabinets lined the walls and a wooden table took up much of the space in the center of the room. The twins and their young families shared this house, while Peter lived with his wife in a smaller home elsewhere on the property.

John came into the kitchen. Pema wasn't surprised to see him, since he often stayed overnight at the farm, and he was sure to want to be present at a family council.

"Sit down, Pema," said Peter. "We have some serious talking to do."

She sat at the table, slightly surprised. Although Peter was the eldest, it was usually the more outgoing John who took the lead at these family conferences. If Peter was concerned enough to bring up the main topic directly, without the pleasant chatting that normally started these conferences, he must be concerned indeed.

"We've been going through the books," Peter said. "The farm is in trouble."

Pema looked from one brother to the next, her green eyes widening. Peter's face was somber, John's held a hint of frustrated anger, but what scared her the most was the despair and helplessness she saw in the twins' blue eyes.

10 LAKE OF DREAMS

"In trouble," she repeated. "What exactly does that mean?"

"We're in debt." John took up the explanation. "You know that, of course, we have been for years, ever since we made the decision to buy the new machinery. But we've had two years of drought since then, our yield has dropped, and it looks like this summer may be just as dry. During this past year, we haven't even been able to keep up with the interest payments."

"Oh, John." Pema's good mood was gone. "How bad is it?" She thought of friends and neighbors, fellow farmers, who over the past few years had lost their farms. They were gone, leaving the land they had loved and nourished, the land that had nourished them.

"We need cash," John said. "We need it in a hurry. But we do have a couple of options. That's why we need to talk today."

Pema nodded.

"Option one," John said. "We can sell some of the land. Discussion?"

Five pairs of eyes, four blue, one green, searched one another to see if anyone had any answers. Finally Peter spoke. "I'm against that. We're just barely holding our own against the larger operations as it is. We all know that the future of farming is going to be bigger farms."

"Yes," said James. "It's mainly the smaller farms that have been forced off the land."

"We need to hang on to all the land we have." Peter's large fist was clenched around his empty coffee mug. "If possible we need to expand."

"We can't expand," John said. "At least not until this current crisis is over." He looked at George, who nodded his agreement, and then at Pema.

LAKE OF DREAMS

"We can't sell the land." Pema's voice was barely a whisper. She hadn't known things had become this serious. She knew that interest rates had been high back when the five of them had agreed to buy the new machinery, but their wheat crops then had been good, and expanding their operation had seemed the wise thing to do. Lose part of the farm?

Pema usually had little to do with the day-to-day running of the farm. The twins and Peter did that, while John, still a bachelor, spent most of his weekends out here. But the farm was part of her. It was in her blood. The land had been Robinson land for generations.

"You said there was another option?" Pema looked at John and then at Peter.

"Yes," said Peter. He stood up and turned to the counter, where a pot of coffee was always keeping warm. His back to her as he filled his mug, he said, "We can sell the lake."

Pema froze.

The twins turned to her, their broad faces eager. "Don't you see?" James said. "It's the perfect solution. We can raise the cash we need without selling any of the farmland."

She looked out the kitchen window. She could see her car silhouetted against the bright sky that arched over the fields, which were filled with young wheat and with hope. For two years now those fields that grew her brothers' dreams had withered and died beneath the scorching sky.

James was right. Selling the lake was the perfect solution. But how could she live without Meniskamee? For while the farm held her brothers' dreams and future, the lake held hers.

John came and sat next to her, putting his arm across her shoulders. Perhaps because he, too, lived in the city, he understood better than his brothers how much the lake meant to her, how she valued those times when she was free to take her canoe and travel there. "Pema," he said. "I wish there was another way. But you yourself said it. We can't sell the land."

"We can't sell Meniskamee." Pema held herself stiffly, but her green eyes were filling with tears. "We've got to think of a third option. And besides—" she turned to John with sudden hope "—who'd want to buy a lake in the middle of northern Saskatchewan?" She gripped John's sleeve, her fingers digging into his muscular forearm, but she felt her hopes fall as he bent his head and looked at the table.

"Actually," he said, "there is someone who's interested. He owns a computer firm in Toronto. He wants to build a retreat."

She stared at him in disbelief. She didn't say anything, in part because there seemed to be nothing to say, and in part because a big lump had suddenly appeared in her throat.

John tightened his arm around her. His body seemed to be saying, "I'm sorry, I know how you feel," but when his mouth opened, what he said was, "He's coming tomorrow to look at the lake. We've arranged to fly him out."

The lump in Pema's throat grew bigger and hotter, until she thought it would choke her. She opened her mouth, trying to take in some air, but instead a sob escaped. She turned from John and, resting her head in her hands, tried to hold back the tears.

Peter came around the table. He put a warm mug of coffee in front of her and placed his hand on her shoulder. "Pema," he said. "I know this seems like we're trying to sell the lake out from under you. We know how much it means to you. But it's the farm we're talking about. You love the farm, too."

She lifted her head. She wrapped her hands around the comfort of the coffee mug. "I know." Her voice wavered, but the tears were held in check.

"We haven't made the final decision yet," Peter said. "At the moment it seems like the best option, but we'll keep trying. All we're asking is that you understand, and wait until this man sees the property. That's all. He may decide he doesn't want to buy it."

Pema nodded. "All right." The tears were beginning to burn behind her eyes again, and she stood up. "I'm going back to the city now."

Her brothers didn't try to stop her, even though the family usually had supper together after one of these meetings. John followed her out to the car. "Thank you," he said. "I know how hard this is for you."

"It's hard for all of us," she said.

John hugged her. "We're a family." He hesitated for a moment, then continued. "As if all this isn't enough, I have a favor to ask. I don't have to work tomorrow and I'd like to stay at the farm tonight. Can you pick up this man at the airport tomorrow?"

Pema stopped, one hand on her car door. "You expect me to help you sell the lake?" John started to say something, his eyes sad, but Pema cut him off. "I know, it's for the family." She sighed. "Okay, I'll pick him up. But I have an exam to give at two. What time is his flight?"

"It's at eleven. I can get into town by one-thirty. Why don't you take him to your apartment and I'll meet you there and bring him out here. His name is Christie."

14 LAKE OF DREAMS

"Okay." Pema got into her car.

The day that had seemed so glorious was now dull and faded. No longer did Pema feel a temptation to exceed the speed limit. In her head, a rhythm repeated itself over and over again. *The farm, the lake, the farm, the lake.* How could she decide? But then she shook herself. She wouldn't dwell on this now. In two days she was leaving for the lake. She and her canoe were going to Meniskamee. Being there always gave her the strength she needed to handle what life dealt. And Grandfather would be there. He would know what she should do.

Michael Christie walked into the arrival area of the airport. "Welcome to Saskatoon, Saskatchewan," he said to himself. He felt a twinge of disappointment that there was no one here to say it to him. What a great line. It would almost be worth living here, just to be able to say "Saskatoon, Saskatchewan" to people. But of course there was no one here to meet him, because John Robinson was expecting him to be on flight 833, which was running an hour and a half late. He had tried phoning John from Toronto when he'd learned he would be on a different flight, but there had been no answer. His luggage, anyway, was on the other plane. So now he was here with time to kill. Well, he could wander around the airport and look in the shops, maybe have a drink.

He put his briefcase down and looked around. Wait a minute. Killing time here was going to be a problem. This airport was just one big room. And there, at the far end, was one baggage carousel. One carousel? For a moment he felt a twinge of homesickness for the busy Toronto airport, with its row after row of baggage pickup areas.

LAKE OF DREAMS

Hold it, stop, he said to himself. Wait a minute, what was this, Michael the big-city snob? And besides, what exactly was he homesick for? An overcrowded airport? Just think of the fun that could be had there, hurrying to find the right place, worrying about similar-looking suitcases, fighting through the press of people all waiting to spot their bags, swinging heavy suitcases off the belts with total disregard for the safety of those standing nearby.

Michael gave himself a mental shake. Getting away from the city was the reason he was looking for the site of the new retreat himself, rather than designating it to one of his staff. Doctor's orders. He had to relax more, go with the flow, even act impulsively once in a while. He picked up his briefcase. It was either that or end up like his father, dead of a heart attack at age forty-eight. He'd wander around and look for a magazine, then go in the airport restaurant and grab something to eat while he waited.

Pema gripped the telephone receiver and tried to keep her voice calm. "John, the plane's late. You have to get here to meet it, because I can't stay too much longer." She listened for a moment, then continued. "They're saying it's due at one now, but first they said fifteen minutes late, then half an hour, and so on. Any minute now they'll announce it's not coming until one-thirty or two, and I have to give that exam at two." John spoke again. "Okay," Pema said, "I'll stay here until you get here or until one-thirty, whichever comes first. But I'll bet you anything that the plane won't get here before I have to leave... Well, no, I won't bet you a month of cleaning your house. Anything else. Bye."

16   LAKE OF DREAMS

She hung up. It was almost noon. Maybe she'd go over to the restaurant and get something to eat.

The little cafeteria was crowded. Pema set her tray on one of the last free tables and sat down to eat her soup and salad. She was wishing she'd brought a book along, anything to help the time go faster, when something made her look up.

A man was standing by the cashier, carrying a coat, a briefcase, several magazines and a full tray. He was looking around for somewhere to sit. Pema's spoon paused midway between her bowl of soup and her mouth as she stared. Wow! she thought. Tall, dark and handsome didn't begin to describe this man. He was big and broad, and even with all he was holding, he stood with a grace that hinted of shadowy jungle and slitted eyes glowing in the night. His hair was dark brown and wavy, and his eyes were a bright emerald green. And right now, oh, those eyes were looking directly at her.

Michael scanned the small room, looking for an empty table, but there wasn't one. Well, he'd just have to share with someone. Someone like that woman there, sitting alone. He'd never seen hair that color, a red so deep, so rich, it was almost the color of mahogany. He started to walk toward her and noticed that she was looking at him. Her eyes were green, but not the vivid green of his own. Hers were like mossy pools, and he felt he could fall into them and drown quite happily. Just then, the tray he was carrying began to tip. His coat and the magazines slipped to the floor as he juggled the tray and managed to get it under control before spilling too much of his lunch. He looked toward the table, figuring he'd put the tray down before he tried to pick everything up, and saw that the woman was standing up.

LAKE OF DREAMS 17

She unfolded gracefully from her chair. Tall, slim, he'd never seen such long legs on a woman. They were perfect. She was wearing olive green corduroys and a tailored tan jacket. Around her neck was a silky wisp of pale green. The ends of the scarf curled gently over her breasts. *She* was perfect.

Pema was not surprised to find herself on her feet. From that moment of eye contact, the voices of the other people around her had faded away to silence. Time slowed. As if in a dream, she took first one step toward him and then another. Her body on automatic pilot, her every sense tuned in to the dark-haired stranger, she knelt to pick up his coat and magazines. Then, her mind only just beginning to function again, she led the way to her table.

He sat down across from her and took a handful of napkins to mop spilled coffee from his tray. Pema watched him. He was a stranger, the features of his face were new, but they were also familiar somehow, as if she'd known him forever. The green of his eyes was so bright, so full of fire. His nose was straight, his cheekbones prominent, and his chin had just the hint of a cleft. And his mouth—his lips were well-defined, looking soft and inviting. He smiled suddenly, revealing a dimple in his right cheek.

"Do you know," he said, "you're the first person I've met with eyes greener than mine?"

The eyes under question widened.

"Whoops." His smile broadened. "That wasn't supposed to be the first thing I said. I'm supposed to say either, 'Thank you for helping me,' or 'Is it okay if I share this table?' I'm not sure which should come first, though. What do you think?"

18 LAKE OF DREAMS

"You're welcome and sure. There, now it doesn't matter." Pema picked up her cup of tea, not because she was thirsty but because it gave her something to do other than stare at him.

"I'm here to kill time," the man said. "How about you?"

"Me, too. I'm here to meet someone, but his plane isn't here yet."

"Meet someone?" Pema looked up again at the way his voice sharpened. "Your husband?" he asked.

She studied him. He was a total stranger. Surely that question was a little personal. But then she smiled. What did it matter? And besides, the man she was to meet was anything but a loved one. He was coming to take her lake away from her. "No," she said, "not a husband, not even a friend."

"Well, good," the man said. "We can kill time together. My name's Michael, by the way." He held out his hand.

Pema reached across the table and put her hand in his. "Nice to meet you, Michael. I'm Pema."

"Pema," he said. "A beautiful name. A name that tastes of exotic spices, that smells of rare wildflowers."

She laughed. Her hand still rested in his, and almost reluctantly she took it back. "Are you a poet?"

"No. Being corny is a good way to kill time."

"I've never tried it."

"Actually, you know, I wasn't."

Pema took a bite of salad. "Wasn't what?"

"Wasn't being corny. Pema really is a beautiful name."

She looked again into his bright eyes and felt herself drawn in. "Thank you," she said.

LAKE OF DREAMS

They sat gazing at one another until Michael looked down and picked up his sandwich. "Tell me," he said, "all about yourself."

"All?"

"All."

"Well, I'm twenty-five years old. I'm a Gemini. Do you want to know my shoe size?" He shook his head, his eyes never leaving her face. "I teach high-school biology here in Saskatoon." She paused, unable to think of anything else to say. What was it about this man? All she wanted to do was stare at him in silence, and she worried that if she started speaking, she'd babble. "Your turn."

Michael grinned. "I'm six foot three, two hundred pounds, a demon on a squash court and a whiz in a hockey arena. Your turn again."

She finished the last of her soup. "I don't know what else to tell you. Let's see. I have four older brothers. I grew up on a farm."

"Tell me your dreams."

"My dreams." Pema looked past Michael, through the doorway of the restaurant. A small bank of video games stood there, and she could hear the beeps and bells, see the flashing lights. Her dreams. Was that a strange question for him to ask? She thought it should be, but it wasn't. From the moment she had first seen him, complete with magazines and tipping tray, she had been living a dream.

"I dream of Canada wild and beautiful as it once was and should be again. I dream of all living things existing together amid mutual respect." She felt a mild surprise at the back of her mind. She didn't speak like this to anyone, sometimes not even to herself. "I have a bachelor's degree in biology. But what I want to do is go back and get a master's, maybe even a PhD. Then I could work for the Wildlife Federation, or the government, and really do something for conservation."

"So why don't you?"

She picked up her tea. Her lids dropped over her eyes. "Oh," she said, "I have to save money. I'd have to decide which is the best school. And all my family are here." She raised her eyes to his. "What about you? What do you dream of?"

Michael drew in a deep breath. "My dreams have been confused lately. I used to dream of what most men in my position dream of, of being successful in my chosen career. I thought my dream was coming true. I work hard and play hard. But lately, well, I don't know. I don't know what I dream of now."

His green gaze met hers. Pema wanted to touch him, wanted to run her fingers down the line of his jaw and rest it on the softness of his lips, wanted to take his hand and intertwine her fingers with his. But they were strangers still, and so she didn't.

They sat silently for a few minutes. Words weren't needed. The sounds of the coffee shop filled the space between them, the hum of voices, the clatter of cutlery. They finished eating, and the talk began to flow again. Pema told Michael about the teachers and students she worked with. Michael kept her laughing with stories about the days when he had played hockey.

"I considered playing professional," he said. Her eyes widened. "Oh, don't be too impressed, I wasn't really all that good. But back then, I thought I was. I was practicing with the Toronto Maple Leafs, and one of the guys checked me into the boards. I'm sure it was just a friendly little check, but I hit my head and was out cold for several minutes."

LAKE OF DREAMS

"How terrible."

"I actually thought of it as a sign from above. Thou shalt not play hockey, you know, something like that. And anyway, it made my parents happy when I told them I'd decided not to play."

"What's your family like?" Pema asked, but just then a voice came over the loudspeakers, announcing a plane had been delayed ten minutes, until one forty-five. She looked at her watch and saw, to her horror, that it was twenty-five to two. "Oh," she gasped, "I've got to run." She jumped up and looked out the restaurant door. She didn't see John, but she had to leave anyway. And besides, she'd been right, the plane she was supposed to meet wasn't due now until two.

She held out her hand to Michael. "You were a wonderful person to kill time with," she said. "Perhaps we'll meet again. I'm sorry to rush off, but I've got an exam to give."

"Wait," Michael said. "I thought you were meeting someone..." But she was gone. He thought of running after her, but her slender form quickly disappeared into the knots of people standing around the baggage carousel. He sat back and realized he didn't even know her last name. Pema. A special name and a very special lady. He'd have liked to spend longer with her, would have liked to see her again. Sighing, he picked up his stack of magazines and began idly turning pages.

When the plane he was supposed to be on was announced, he went out to where the people arriving came through. Here was a game. Could he spot John Robinson? Let's see, that tall, skinny man over there? No, he looked too sour to have been the enthusiastic voice he had heard over the telephone. That man in the tweed

22   LAKE OF DREAMS

jacket? Maybe. Whoops, no, not if he was greeting the pretty woman carrying a baby. Aha.

Michael made his way over to a man dressed in jeans and a sports jacket, his broad face open and honest. "John Robinson?" he said.

"That's me." The man grinned, deepening lines worn in his face by sun and wind. "Michael Christie? We sure are glad you could come all this way to see our lake."

"Your lake sounds like it's exactly what I've been looking for." Michael shook John's hand. The two moved to the side, away from the crowds of people who hurried by, searching faces and hugging loved ones.

"We hope so," said John. "There's been a change of plan, though."

"If the lake and cabin are what I want," Michael said, "I'm sure we'll be able to solve any problems."

"I'm certain, too, that we can work something out, but the first thing will be getting you there."

"Aren't you flying me out to see it, as we agreed?" Michael asked. "And why don't we talk over by the baggage carousel. I always like to be sure my luggage has arrived in the same city."

"There's no hurry," John said. "It always takes the guys a while to unload the planes. But sure, we can go over there."

As John had predicted, while the carousel was already turning around and around, its polished metal panels were empty of any luggage.

"About this problem," John said. "I know we said we'd fly you out. But there's a lot of forest fires up north. We've had no rain for weeks. Bad for fires, and for farmers, too." John stuck his big fists into his jacket pockets, causing the jacket to ball out at his waist. "We had a float plane reserved to fly you to the lake. The pi-

LAKE OF DREAMS

lot called this morning. He's got two planes he rents out. The Cessna's blown a cylinder, and the Beaver's been drafted by the local resources officer to fly fire fighters into the bush. But we've arranged another way for you to get out to the lake."

Michael studied John. He figured the Saskatchewan man was about his own age, thirty-four. John's skin was seamed and reddened, his hands work-roughened. He also seemed uncomfortable. Michael had a feeling that whatever the alternate form of transportation to the lake was, John wasn't too happy about it.

"If there is another way to get me to the lake," Michael said, "then there's no problem."

"Oh, getting you there's no problem," John said. "You can go by canoe. It's my sister that's the problem."

Michael put his briefcase between his feet. This guy seemed to have something mixed up. He saw no reason a sister should be a problem. But a canoe certainly *was*. "You expect me to travel by canoe?"

"Sure. It's an easy trip. Take you about three days. But my sister, well . . ."

Michael stopped listening. He was in shock. Sit in a canoe for three days? Was this man crazy? Canoes leaked. They tipped over. He'd rather be checked into the boards by an entire hockey team than subject himself to three days of unnecessary torture.

John put a hand on Michael's forearm and gripped it with surprising strength. Michael tuned in.

"So you see," John was saying, "we're hoping you'll be able to convince her. This canoe trip is really a blessing in disguise. You can help her get used to the idea that selling the lake seems to be our only option."

24 LAKE OF DREAMS

"Wait a minute," Michael said. "I'm going to be traveling for three days in a canoe with your sister?"

"She's a real good outdoorswoman. She takes kids out on trips all the time. You don't need to worry."

Michael sighed. "Well, this certainly isn't what I'd expected." He looked at John, at the faded blue eyes that were pleading so eloquently in their silence for him to understand, and realized that this was the best that could be done. He thought about the lake, which really did sound ideal. And he could afford to take the extra days. Be impulsive, he told himself.

"That lake," he said, "sounds exactly like what I want. Since I came all this way, I may as well go and look at it. There's no problem."

John broke into a large grin. "I'm glad you see it that way. We're all set for you to leave tomorrow. You can stay at the farm tonight. And as for my sister, I'm sure she'll be no trouble. She's a good girl."

Good girl, I'm sure, thought Michael. An outdoorswoman, eh? She probably dresses in flannel shirts and army boots. But just then the first piece of luggage slid onto the carousel, and he put the Robinson sister out of his mind.

Pema lay in her bed that night and felt as if she was floating. Thoughts of the man at the airport, Michael, had been in her head all through the exam she had given. She'd had a hard time marking it that evening because his green eyes and grin kept looking up at her from the papers. Now, in her bed, he was still with her.

This is silly, she thought. He's just a stranger I spent a little time with. In fact, maybe that's why we were able to talk so freely, because we knew we'd never see each

LAKE OF DREAMS   25

other again. But she couldn't stop thinking about him. Maybe they would meet again. She'd like that.

At least the meeting with him had stopped her from fretting over the possibility that the family would have to sell Meniskamee. It was much better to think about the handsome green-eyed stranger than to think of what she would do if she could never go to the lake again.

Today, with Michael, she felt she had met someone she could really be herself with, someone who would take her as she was. There had only been one other person in her life who had seen her for what she was, who had accepted her and encouraged her solely on the basis of her own traits and abilities. Grandfather. She felt tears come to her eyes. Boy, this certainly was an emotional night. She sat up in bed and reached for a tissue. There was no need to cry. Grandfather was gone in body, but she knew that he had not truly left her alone. He was always there if she needed him, especially at the lake. Oh, how she was looking forward to setting off on the canoe trip the next day.

She lay back again, and thought more about Michael. One thing about him, he was so big, he almost made her feel small. Five feet ten made for a very tall woman. Too tall, she used to think. But Grandfather had helped her see that her height was part of who she was, and that since she couldn't hide it, she might as well use it to her advantage.

"Walk tall," he had told her, "walk proud. When you walk as if you own the earth, people believe you do." And then he had smiled and his brown face had creased into a network of fine wrinkles. "And besides, a big woman is a strong woman. You are better able to portage your canoe and camp in the bush because of it."

26   LAKE OF DREAMS

And so Pema did walk tall. And when she swung an ax to break up dead wood for her camp fire, or shouldered her pack before rolling her canoe onto her back, she was glad for her sturdy frame. But sometimes she still wondered if she could be considered feminine.

Despite her thoughts and dreams, she slept well and was up early to pack for her trip.

Pema kept her canoe at the farm, as there was no room for it in her one-bedroom apartment. And besides, if it was where she could see it every day, it would sing its song of river and lake to her and she would be filled with longing to be out in the bush.

Her gear was at the farm, too, under her canoe in its special low shed. She dressed, taking the time to wrap one of her favorite scarves around her head, and grabbed an apple and a piece of bread to eat in the car while driving to the farm.

She kept the car at a steady pace. Despite her joy at the thought that she was finally to set off for the lake, she couldn't help wondering if it was still her lake. If this man had arrived yesterday, he was probably on his way there this morning. Maybe John had driven him to the airstrip yesterday, and they were at the lake at this very moment. If that was the case, then the man might be telling John right now that he would love to buy it. Pema knew anyone who saw Meniskamee couldn't help but be enchanted by it. If the man saw it, he would want to buy it. And what would she do then?

She parked in front of the farmhouse and went inside. To her surprise, the first person she saw was John. "What are you doing here?" she asked. "I thought you'd be with the man from Toronto, on your way to the lake."

LAKE OF DREAMS

"Hi," John said. He turned. "Pema's here," he called through the doorway that led from the kitchen. He turned back, smiled and picked up a paper napkin from the countertop.

Pema began to get the impression that something was a little strange. For one thing, neither of the twins' wives were in the kitchen. This time in the morning they were always in here, usually with several children underfoot. And John was standing there, a nervous grin on his face, his hands busily shredding the napkin.

Her brothers came in. When they were all seated at the table, John said, "We've had a problem. We weren't able to use the plane to fly the man up to the lake."

"Oh." She felt a faint flame of hope. Maybe he wouldn't get to see Meniskamee after all. "Did he go back to Toronto?"

"No." It was Peter who answered. "He's here. Upstairs."

"Oh," she said again. A terrible thought had just entered her mind. "Then how are you planning to get him to the lake?"

The brothers looked at one another for inspiration. None was there. John took a deep breath. "We thought, since you were heading that way, you could take him."

"What!" Pema sprang to her feet. "Yesterday you wanted me to pick him up from the airport. Now you want me to escort him to the lake?"

"Pema, we're sorry." John stood up, too. "We know how hard this is for you. But we're all in this together. We have to think what's best for the farm, for the family. At the moment, it seems like selling the lake is our only option. We hope we don't have to. All we're asking is that you take this man along and let him have a look at it."

28   LAKE OF DREAMS

Pema stood very still. "This is possibly my last trip to the lake. Now you want to take that away from me, too?"

Her brothers were all watching her. She looked into the four faces and saw love and sorrow there. But she also saw pity. And a small flame began to burn deep within her chest.

"You've all decided, haven't you? You've decided that the only way to save the farm is to sell the lake. You're not even going to try to think of another way. I hope you realize I'm not the best person to deliver a powerful sales pitch to this man."

John put a hand on her arm. "It's not like that, Pema, really. We don't want to sell the lake. We know you love it, and we love you. But—"

"I'm trying to adjust, I really am." Pema shook his arm off and turned to look out the window. "I'm trying to get used to the idea that this could be my last trip to Meniskamee. But it won't be the same if I have to take some stranger along."

Her heart was a heavy lump in her chest. She turned to face her brothers. They watched her in silence. This wasn't easy for them, either. She forced a smile to her lips. "This would almost be funny," she said, "if I didn't feel so sad. Can you picture me canoeing with a man from Toronto? He's probably a yuppie. He won't know which end of a paddle is up. And how's he going to manage camping? He'll worry about getting his designer jeans wrinkled. He'll be upset if the color of the lake clashes with his tie. He won't consider leaving civilization without taking along his microwave oven and a supply of imported mineral water!"

Pema knew her attempt to use humor to fight her pain wasn't working. She definitely didn't feel like laughing,

LAKE OF DREAMS

and her brothers didn't laugh, either. In fact, they were acting very strangely. They were fidgeting, making strange faces at her, waving their hands at her. Now she saw that they were all staring at a point somewhere behind her.

She whirled. There, in the kitchen doorway, stood Michael.

Chapter Two

Michael had been there for several minutes. He'd come downstairs, looking for breakfast, and heard voices in the kitchen. When he reached the doorway, he realized the conversation in progress was probably not one he should interrupt, but before he could retreat, he saw Pema.

It was her, the woman from the airport. She was the Robinson sister. No flannel shirts or army boots there! She looked lovely, dressed in shades of brown. An emerald scarf was tied around her temples, and its long ends streamed down the side of her head, mingling with the flow of red hair that cascaded, loose and free, down her back. But then the words she was saying began to sink in.

She didn't want to take him in her canoe to see the lake. Admittedly, he didn't want to go in her canoe to see the lake, but he had come all this way to see it. And now it was becoming a challenge. Michael liked challenges.

LAKE OF DREAMS   31

The more obstacles that were set in his way when he wanted something, the more determined he became to reach his goal. He had decided not to let the physical discomfort of canoeing stand in his way. Now he wouldn't let this woman stand in his way, either.

But she didn't want to sell the lake. He began to understand a little more of what John had been talking about yesterday. She didn't want to sell, but the family needed the money to save the farm. It seemed that she didn't really have much choice.

He mulled this over until Pema began to speak of her opinion of people from Toronto. Boy, he might have been a bit of a big-city snob in the airport yesterday, but she was just as bad. He felt a small anger beginning to burn. But then he smiled wryly. He realized that he was angry, in part, because what she was saying rang a bit too true. He *had* been concerned about the discomforts of the trip. He hadn't wanted to admit his ignorance about canoeing. He'd even wondered if he could bring his portable CD player along. But he wasn't going to let all this stop him. He was here to see the lake, and see the lake he would. And so, when Pema whirled to face him, he ignored the pain in her eyes.

"Are there any problems with my getting out to see the lake?" he asked.

"No." John leaped to his feet. "We're just having a small family disagreement. You know how families are. Please, come and sit down. What would you like to eat?"

Michael did not respond. He stayed in the doorway, his green gaze never leaving Pema.

She felt rooted to the spot. Here was Michael, the man from the airport, the man she had dreamed of all night long. They had met again. But this man to whom she had felt so close so quickly had come to take her lake away from her.

John led Michael to the table. George brought him a cup of coffee, and James went to find his wife to come and make breakfast.

Pema's eyes followed Michael as he crossed the room, but then she turned abruptly. "I'm going to put the canoe on the car. Is he packed and ready?"

"Actually," said Michael, "I'm not packed and ready. I didn't expect a canoe trip, and so I don't have the right clothes. I don't even know exactly what I should be packing."

"Don't worry, Pema will help you," Peter said.

Pema stared at the men sitting around the table, at the twins' wives who had come in and were bustling around fixing breakfast. Then she bolted from the room.

She ran to the long, low shed where she kept her canoe. Ducking, she entered the building and sank to the dirt floor next to the canoe. It was lying, hull up, on special rests she had made, and she leaned her forehead against its cool, smooth surface.

It looked as if she was taking Michael along whether she wanted to or not. Part of her wanted to. Hadn't she been hoping to meet him again? But he was going to buy her lake. He was going to take her dream away.

Wait a minute. She sat up. He didn't know anything about canoeing. Perhaps if he discovered just how uncomfortable and inconvenient the trip to the lake was, he would see Meniskamee really wasn't the right place to build his retreat. If he learned firsthand of the demands on muscles made by paddling a canoe, of the discomforts of sleeping on the ground and of dealing with blackflies and mosquitoes . . .

LAKE OF DREAMS 33

A smile curved her lips. But then she looked down and the smile vanished. What if he didn't buy the lake because of something she did, and then the family did have to sell some of the farmland?

"What do I do now?" she said aloud. She stroked the hull, remembering how she and her grandfather had built the mold to shape the lengthwise strips of wood that formed the canoe. He had helped her lay the fiberglass cloth over it. His hands had shown her how to smooth on the resin. Under his direction, she had sanded the fiberglass until it was completely transparent, so that the beauty of the wood shone through.

"This isn't exactly your ancestors' method of building a canoe," Grandfather had said. "But it will give you a craft that is light and strong. It will sing in the water for you, my Pema, because it will sense the love you bear for the country you will travel together."

Grandfather. He was Métis, of Indian and French blood, and to Pema he would always be the wise and gentle man who knew everything anyone needed to know. Now, as she stroked the canoe that hands—hers and his—had made, she seemed to hear him say, *Pema, it will be all right. Take your canoe and go to the lake. Take the man with you. I will be there waiting for you both. Remember, love is what matters, and you, my child, know love.*

Pema stood and began to slide the canoe along its padded rests out of the shed. Grandfather was right, as always. She would do as she had to do.

Once the canoe was on the car, she gathered her gear and took it into the kitchen to pack. Michael was there, trying on a heavy wool shirt that belonged to George.

Pema glanced up from checking that her first-aid kit was complete, and found herself looking at Michael's bare torso. The roll of surgical tape fell from her fingers unnoticed. His chest was covered with a mat of curling dark hair that tapered into a vee as it disappeared beneath his belt buckle. He turned to say something to Peter, and the muscles of his back rippled as he reached out to take another shirt.

She swallowed, her mouth suddenly dry, and stuffed all the first-aid items into their waterproof bag. "I'll have to borrow some food from you," she said to George. "I didn't bring enough fresh stuff for two. And you—" she jerked her chin toward Michael "—I hope you have some heavy pants and thick socks. You'll need to keep covered because of the blackflies and mosquitos."

Michael looked as if he was wondering, not for the first time, what exactly he was letting himself in for, but he said, "You needn't worry about me. Your brothers are lending me the things I don't have."

"Good." Pema held up one of the packs. "This will be yours. I'm putting the heavier stuff in your pack, since I'll be carrying my pack and portaging the canoe."

Michael's lips tightened. "I'm sure I'll be quite capable of carrying whatever will be necessary, including the canoe." A yellow spark flared in his eyes, and Pema felt a chill. For a moment, she was lost in a jungle, the hair rising on the back of her neck, knowing she was being stalked by a hard-muscled shadow.

She looked down from the green fire of his gaze and put her repair kit and cooking utensils into her pack. She stuffed the dishwashing gear, flashlight and candles into the pack, and checked that the compass and maps in their waterproof coverings were ready for when she needed them. And she blinked back the burning sensa-

LAKE OF DREAMS

tion behind her eyes. She had so looked forward to being alone, just her and her canoe, and now it wasn't going to happen.

Once all the equipment was packed, she put the food into the other pack. Michael was trying on various pairs of her brothers' boots. "It's lucky," said Peter, "that you're so similar in size to us."

"Yeah," said John, "you could almost be one of the family."

Pema stood up and swung the food pack onto Michael's lap. She wanted to remove any thoughts of that sort from her brothers' heads. "I'll get changed. Are you almost ready?"

"He'll be ready," said John. "These boots are fine. I'll get a cap for you, Michael."

Pema carried the last of her things for the trip. She had changed into a pair of tan jeans and a brown T-shirt with green leaves all over it. The thin cotton material clung to her long, slim waist, and molded itself over her high breasts. Michael watched as she twisted her hair into a knot at her neck and secured it with a clip. She tied a brown scarf around her neck and placed a small pile of other scarves into her pack. Doing up the leather clasps on the pack, she slung it over one shoulder and asked, "Are you ready?"

She started to brush by him on her way out to the car but he caught her wrist with his long fingers. His eyes swept her face as if searching for something, but she couldn't tell if he found it.

"I'm ready," he said softly.

Pema and Michael sat side by side in her small car. They had been driving for over an hour now, and neither had said a word. Pema pressed the button on the radio for the twentieth time, changing the station. She stared straight out the windshield, watching the familiar highway roll by. She was filled with a terrible fear. What if she lost the lake? All her dreams of graduate school would mean nothing then. Without the research she planned to do at the lake, she wouldn't be able to get her degree. She knew how much her family needed the money that the sale of the property would bring. The farm was her brothers' lives. How could she deny them the money they needed? But without the lake... Well, she wouldn't think about it. With this man here beside her, though, she couldn't help but think of it.

Michael was looking out the window, watching the fields of wheat and canola go by. Pema's senses were so tuned to him that she felt, rather than saw, each time he turned his head to look at her, his gaze steady as if he was studying the inside of her head. Then he reached forward and switched the radio off. "Hello," he said. "My name is Michael. It's nice to meet you."

"Are you going to tell me to have a nice day?" she asked.

"No," he said. "I'd just be wasting my breath. But you could have a better day. Would it cheer you up if I expressed my total ignorance about this trip? That way I could ask you questions, and you could answer them and feel superior."

Despite herself, Pema felt her lips stretch into a smile. "I'd love to feel superior. Ask away."

"Well, first of all, where are we going?"

"Oh." Her smile grew larger. "I suppose you must feel you're being whisked off into the unknown."

"Exactly. Here I am, expecting to be flown in comfort in a plane to view a lake, and now..."

LAKE OF DREAMS

At the mention of the lake, Pema's face hardened. It had been there again, the attraction she felt for the stranger in the airport. But she mustn't forget, couldn't let herself forget, he was not who she had thought he was.

"Okay," he said, "question number one. Where are we driving to?"

"Breton Lake. That's where we start canoeing." She didn't want to think about Meniskamee, and hearing him talk about it as if it was a piece of meat on display in a market made her feel like crying. "It'll take us until late afternoon to get there. Normally I'm more than halfway by now, but we got a late start."

Michael glanced at her to see if her words were meant to be barbed, but her face, as she attended to her driving, was open.

"We'll have to see," she continued, "if there'll be time when we get there to do a couple of hours of canoeing. We won't make it to where I usually camp, but I know of other sites. And, of course, I'll have to give you a canoe lesson."

"Thank you, I'd appreciate that."

This time it was Pema who glanced over to see if sarcasm lay behind Michael's words, but he only grinned at her.

"Can you teach a complete beginner enough to canoe in such a short time?" he asked.

"There really isn't a lot to learn. How to hold your paddle, how to stroke. How to get in and out of a canoe. How to load it. You'll be in the bow, at least at first, so you don't need to know anything about steering. I'd like to get you in the stern eventually, though. The canoe handles better with more weight in the back."

"Tell me more about canoeing."

38 LAKE OF DREAMS

"It's the only way to travel." Pema's eyes softened. "It's the only natural way. A motorboat may be quicker, but you're polluting the air with noise and fumes. A sailboat is natural, too, but in it you're at the mercy of winds. In a canoe, it's really just you and the water and the bush. You go where you want, you are silent, you're part of it all." She looked at Michael, not quite daring to believe that this city man could understand.

"I think I see," he said. "You like the feeling that you're a natural being traveling through the natural environment in as nonintrusive a way as possible."

She gave him a radiant smile. "You do understand. When I'm canoeing, I feel I'm truly a part of the world I'm passing through. I belong there, I'm accepted. And that's how it should be, you know." Her words began to come in a rush, tumbling over one another. "Man is a living being like all other beings. It's wrong, artificial, for him to have removed himself from his environment."

"Would you have us go back to the Stone Age?" Michael asked. "Give up all the technology that has given us healthier, better lives?"

"No, of course not. But it's the attitude that all these so-called benefits of civilization have fostered that I object to. Man has lost all respect for the world he lives in. And he needs that world. He needs the resources it has to offer."

"Exactly," Michael broke in. "He needs them, so he has to take them."

"But he takes them without thinking of the future. He takes them without thinking of the others who share them, too. All that motivates industrialists and businessmen is profit. It doesn't matter what happens to the world as long as they make the biggest profit possible."

LAKE OF DREAMS 39

"Now wait a minute. Like it or not, money is what runs our civilization. Without the chance to make money, no one would be motivated enough to—"

"That's the problem." Pema's hands tightened on the steering wheel. "Just because it is that way doesn't mean it's right. It's not. It doesn't have to be that way. Take the native people who used to live on this land. They lived in harmony with their land. They believed every living thing had a spirit. They took only what they needed, and they apologized to the spirits for needing to kill."

Michael watched her. Her moss green eyes were luminous in their excitement. He enjoyed intellectual argument, but there was something more going on here. There was a radiant beauty in the depths of Pema that he was only just beginning to understand.

She took a deep breath and tried to relax her fingers. "I'm sorry," she said. "I know I sound like I'm up on a soapbox. But it's just so important to me. People are living in an environment and a way of life totally foreign to their spirits. And I truly believe all people feel the stresses of living in an unnatural way."

Michael didn't answer. He was thinking of his own life-style and of the reasons he was sitting in this car, driving north through Saskatchewan.

"Why do you want the lake, anyway?" Pema asked. "Your company's in Toronto, you and all your employees live in Toronto. Why would you want an isolated lake in the middle of Saskatchewan?"

He sighed. "We have a branch in Vancouver. Saskatchewan is an ideal location because it's in the middle." He paused, glancing out the window. "My employees want a retreat. The work we do involves a lot of sitting in front of computer screens. We built a fit-

40 LAKE OF DREAMS

ness center in our office. But at one of our monthly meetings we realized it wasn't enough.''

She nodded and slowed the car as a driver ahead signaled a turn. It sounded as if Michael's company was one in which employees at every level had an equal voice. She liked that.

''We need a place to go where we can escape from the daily pressures of the business,'' he was saying. ''The most important aspect of our work is developing new products. We need a place to brainstorm, a place away from our usual environment, so our minds can be free to explore new ideas. An isolated place, especially a beautiful one like your lake, would be ideal.''

They drove in silence for a time, passing through the town of Prince Albert. Pema thought about what Michael had said. She was interested to hear him admit that even a Toronto man like himself needed to get closer to a natural environment. It was a good cause, but it didn't make it any easier to think of losing her lake. What about her needs for that natural environment?

As they came out of the town, a car coming the other way began to signal a left turn. It slowed and waited until Pema passed before making the turn.

''You know,'' she said, her voice soft, ''sometimes it amazes me that cars coming the other way actually stop to let me pass. It seems almost as if I'm invisible, and so they shouldn't be able to see me. And it's a surprise when they do.''

Pema was driving with her left hand on the wheel. Her right lay loosely in her lap. Michael reached over and traced the back of her hand with his finger. When she didn't stiffen or move it away, he covered it with his own. ''Pema,'' he said, ''I'm not surprised that they see you.

LAKE OF DREAMS 41

The whole world can see you. You're a very special, radiant person.''

She looked at him in surprise. Her thoughts were tumbled and confused. Why had she come out with that silly little fear of hers? It was just that sometimes she felt she had so little control over her life, so little impact on the world, it was as if she didn't exist.

At least Michael hadn't laughed at her. But who was he, anyway? First impressions are lasting, she reminded herself. Yesterday her first impression had been so wonderful. She'd felt a bond between them. Today she'd learned that he had come here to take her lake. So why did she still feel that she could talk to him and he would understand?'

"Tell me about the country we'll be canoeing through," said Michael.

"We start on Breton Lake. We go only a little way before we turn off onto a river. Maribel River.''

"Do we catch our supper in the river?''

"We can. The best place to fish is right where the river empties into the lake. We can probably camp there tonight. Tomorrow we'll spend most of the morning on the river. Then there's a portage and we get onto Big Wave Lake. It's called that because—''

"Wait, let me guess." Laughter squeezed out with Michael's words. "It's called that because there are big waves on it, right?''

"Well, actually—''

"No, how silly of me." His eyes were dancing. "It's called Big Wave because the lake is the ancient site of the Indian tribes' yearly get-together. And when the powwow was over, and they all parted to go their separate ways, they would wave goodbye to each other. I can see it, the entire shore of the lake, covered with sad people,

42   LAKE OF DREAMS

all waving goodbye. And since it was far across the lake from one shore to another, they had to wave very hard to be seen. Great big waves.''

Pema burst out laughing. "Actually, the big wave is a type of fish, found only in that particular lake. It's twenty feet long, with a triple row of needle teeth. It likes to take bites out of the bottom of canoes, in hopes that something tasty might fall out.''

He smiled, and she continued her description of the trip. "Big Wave is called that because it's often very windy there. The lake is long, and the wind sweeps along it, building up the whitecaps. We'll camp near the end of the lake that night. The next day we portage onto Laughing Spirit River.''

"I won't even try to guess where that name came from.''

"It's because of the white water, especially the series of rapids near where we leave the river. Some people say the name comes from the sound of the water, that it sounds like laughter as it bubbles and runs. But other people say the spirit is laughing because of all the people he has trapped in the rapids, all the canoes he has dumped, all the gear he has soaked. We'll portage around the rapids. The river empties into Clarendon Lake, which takes us to Desiree River, which leads into my lake.''

She fell silent, gazing into the distance. Michael was about to say something when she spoke again.

"Meniskamee Lake. You paddle along Desiree, which is very narrow, and trees grow thickly on either bank, so that you move silently under an archway of trees. The light is always green and silver there. And then, suddenly, the way opens before you, and you come out onto the lake, onto Meniskamee. It's a small lake, almost

LAKE OF DREAMS

round, but the shoreline is formed of many coves and bays. The largest bay has a sandy beach, and that's where Grandfather built his cabin. Trees grow almost to the shore all around the lake. Across from the cabin a big stone outcrop rises, and if you swim there, you can find caves at water level. In some of them, you can hold your breath, swim underwater and come up in an air pocket completely surrounded by stone. One of them has ledges in the rock wall, and that's where I used to keep my treasures.''

Pema fell silent, lost in her image of her lake, until she turned the car into a gravel parking area in front of a small wooden building. "We'll eat here. The food is good.''

Michael got out of the car silently. He could still feel the wisps of the images she had drawn for him coiling through his mind.

"I owe the lake and those who live there a lot," Pema said softly. She stood by the car, one hand still on her door. "The fish, the birds, the animals, the trees. And I'm going to do something for them. I'm going to show how perfectly they all fit together, how completely they belong to the land and the water, and to one another. I will do the research there at the lake, and when I write it up..." Her voice trailed off. She began to walk across the parking area, her footsteps crunching.

That research would never be done now, she thought. She wouldn't share the secrets of the life that was so abundant at the lake. Not if Michael did what he had come here to do. Here she was telling him things she rarely spoke of to anyone, and he would make it all impossible.

She looked up and saw a hawk circling over a nearby field. It plunged suddenly, diving toward the earth with

44   LAKE OF DREAMS

its talons outstretched. Pema braced herself, listening for the squeal of the hawk's intended prey, but heard nothing.

"How can it be you?" she asked Michael. "You were on that plane, the one that was late. How can you be both the man in the airport restaurant and the man who was coming to see my lake?"

"The marvels of modern airline transportation," he said. "When there are connections to be made and overbooked flights, anything's possible." He grinned at her confused look. "I was at a conference in St. John's, Newfoundland, and flew to Saskatoon from there. Thanks to a complicated schedule of flights, and getting bumped from one flight, I ended up on a plane that got me to Saskatoon a little later than the one I was supposed to be on, but that really got me there early, since the other one was late."

Pema was still confused. "Never mind," she said, when he began to explain further, "it doesn't matter. But I wish you and the man in the restaurant weren't the same person."

As she turned and continued toward the restaurant, the hawk rose once again into the air, its claws empty.

They sat in a booth, facing each other. Pema looked at the menu. Nothing looked good. She realized she wasn't very hungry.

"Hey," Michael said. He put a finger under her chin and tipped her head up so she was looking at him. "I'm glad the man in the restaurant is the same man as the one on the plane. And I'm glad you met the one in the shop first. You wouldn't have talked to me the way you did if you'd known who I was. We wouldn't have become friends."

LAKE OF DREAMS   45

Friends? She thought back to that time, only yesterday, when she and Michael had sat at the little table littered with all his magazines. She remembered his open smile and the way his green eyes had focused so attentively on her when she had described her dreams. He was right, they had been friends then. But what were they now?

"I'm still that man," he said. He had lowered his finger from her chin, but she could still feel the warmth of his touch. "And besides, you may have thought I was a terrible Toronto yuppie, but I thought you wore shapeless flannel shirts."

"What?" Despite herself, Pema began to smile.

"Your brother told me what an outdoorswoman you are. The picture of you I formed in my mind included army boots."

"Army boots!"

"So we're even," he said. "We both had misconceptions about each other. Mineral water and army boots. Why don't we just pretend that we're the two people who were getting to know each other yesterday? Pretend that we're friends?"

"Okay," Pema said. She wanted that. But even as she agreed, she wondered. The man she had met at the airport was someone she wanted to be friends with, someone she wanted to know better. But how could she separate him from the man who might take her lake away from her?

By late afternoon they reached the end of the highway portion of their trip. Michael had plenty of time to think during the final hours of the ride, and he spent most of the time torturing himself with visions of what canoeing and camping would be like. He saw himself sitting, wet and cramped, in a teetering, frail craft. He felt the bugs crawling up his pant legs, heard them whining around his head. He saw himself trying to sleep, hearing noises and wondering which of them was the bear who was about to rip a new doorway into his tent.

Pema turned the car off the main road, drove along a dirt track for a couple of miles, then parked the car in a small turnoff near the shore of a lake. She got out and began untying the canoe from the roof of the car.

Michael got out, too, and watched her. This was it, the end of the road. Literally. From here on, the road would be water, not nice solid ground.

Pema finished untying the canoe and tossed the ropes into the car. She slid the canoe to the edge of the roof rack and, standing sideways to it, pulled it until it rested on her shoulders. She carried it across a grassy beach to where a small dock jutted into the water. In a motion almost too quick for him to follow, she had the canoe off her shoulders and resting across her thighs over her bent knees. She lowered the canoe until it lay, upside-down, at the end of the dock. Then she returned to the car for the packs.

Michael carried one of the packs to the dock. As he stepped onto it, he had a sudden feeling of disorientation. Had the ground moved? Looking down, he discovered that the dock was not firmly anchored to the lake bed. It was nothing more than planks of wood resting on large metal barrels. The whole thing was floating, gently rising and falling with the water of the lake. He stood near the land end of it, angry with himself for his shock. He would be floating, or at least he hoped he would be floating and not sinking, for most of the next three days. He'd better get used to it.

LAKE OF DREAMS

Something whined close to his ear, and he waved his hand in the air beside his head. The bugs were after him. Already. Well, that was something else it seemed he would also have to get used to.

Pema brought the last pack and the paddles and dumped them at the end of the dock. Rolling the canoe over, she lowered it into the water. It rested lightly on the surface of the lake. Sunlight sparkled on the rippling water, glinting in his eyes. The canoe looked very small and unstable.

Pema sat on the dock, her feet dangling in the canoe, keeping it from floating away. "Well," she said, waving her hand at the canoe, "get in."

Chapter Three

Michael walked to the end of the dock and looked at the canoe. Pema held a paddle up to him and he took it. The wood was smooth and hard. A flying Canada goose had been painted onto the blade of the paddle, under a coat of varnish.

"Go on," she said. "Sit down with your feet hanging in the canoe, place the paddle across the gunwales and step onto the center line."

He glanced at her. He crouched, then sat beside her. Leaning forward, he placed his paddle across the canoe and, putting weight on it with his hands, stepped into the canoe. The craft rocked and bobbed, but the paddle distributed his weight evenly and the canoe remained stable. He sat on the seat and looked up at her with a grin.

Pema felt her heart lurch. His thick dark hair had fallen forward over his forehead, and the green of his eyes shone out from just beneath it. He looked incredi-

LAKE OF DREAMS

bly pleased with himself. She felt her own mouth begin to stretch into a smile. She turned away and reached for her paddle.

She lowered herself into the canoe so she was facing him and began the lesson. "You are sitting on the stern seat, and I'm in the bow."

"I take it," said Michael, "that normally the two paddlers do not face each other. It would be hard work, paddling in opposite directions."

"I'm sitting this way because it's the easiest way to demonstrate how to paddle."

"I'm grateful." His eyes were teasing her. "And this way I also get a chance to gaze into your lovely face."

Pema felt a blush beginning to stain her cheeks. Why did he say things like that? She dug her paddle into the water. The canoe gave a sudden lurch, and Michael grabbed the gunwales.

"It's more stable," she said, "if the paddlers kneel. You lean your backside against the seat. When the canoe is loaded, especially since there're two of us, it will be riding lower and so will be pretty stable. We can sit up if we need to, but it's usually a good idea to keep one knee down. You switch knees as you switch paddling sides."

The canoe was moving smoothly away from the dock. Michael knelt down. He could feel the little surge of speed with each of Pema's strokes. The motions of her upper body were fluid and contained. Her arms were graceful, and yet he could sense the strength in them as they plunged the paddle into the water, pulled it back, then lifted and swung it forward. The only sound was the drip of the water running off the paddle as she pulled it out of the lake to end each stroke.

50 LAKE OF DREAMS

Her face had softened. She seemed to have forgotten the presence of the man sitting opposite her. To Michael it was as if the wooden craft holding them had become an extension of the woman's lithe body, and she and it were one. And he envied her.

Pema felt the rhythm of her body movements, heard the canoe singing beneath her. Her paddle was alive in her hands, tugging at the water, gliding smoothly through the air. At last the waiting was done. She was here, where she belonged, where she was truly herself. No more city stresses. No more students. No more papers to mark. But wait. She wasn't free at all. Her paddle faltered as she plunged it into the water. The water swirled around the paddle held so still, and the canoe swung in a circle and slowed. Pema's eyes, which had been filled only with water and sky, focused on Michael.

They had come a long way into the lake. The dock was a brown smudge against the green of the shoreline. Michael watched as the light faded from Pema's face and felt like crying out in protest. Watching her had been like watching a bird who has suddenly discovered it has wings. They stared at each other for a moment, surrounded by silence and water. Then she lifted her paddle and showed him how to hold his.

They returned to the dock, Michael propelling the canoe, Pema paddling backward once in a while to keep them in a straight line. Michael felt pleased with himself. He had quickly caught on to the basic paddling stroke and found that the motion of his body felt good. Pema had told him that the next day she would show him the stroke he needed to sit in the stern and steer.

They got out of the canoe and loaded the packs. Pema tossed a life jacket to Michael. She slid the extra paddle

LAKE OF DREAMS

and the fishing rods in under the thwarts. "I hope you aren't too hungry," she said. "I'd like to get in a couple of hours of paddling before we make camp."

They'd had a late lunch, so he wasn't hungry. He glanced at his watch and was surprised to see it was already past what he considered his usual suppertime. He looked into the sky, at the sun, which was nowhere near the horizon.

She smiled. "We're quite far north. It won't get dark for some time still."

They got into the canoe, Michael in the bow facing forward, Pema in the stern. As they started, she felt the rush of excitement she always felt when beginning a trip. She wasn't going to let her fears spoil this trip for her. She was in her canoe and on her way to Meniskamee. And Grandfather would be there. He would know what to do.

She watched Michael. His broad shoulders rotated as he moved his paddle forward to begin a stroke. His arms plunged downward, and she could see the muscles tauten in his shoulders and back as he pulled the paddle through the water. He looked good. She hated to admit it, but he looked as if he belonged. For a city person, he had certainly picked up the rudiments of paddling a canoe very quickly. Of course he was athletic. One could tell that from his build.

Her eyes roamed over him freely. His dark hair curled over the back of his neck. His black T-shirt clung snugly to him. She could see the indentation of his spine as it ran down his back before disappearing beneath the belt of his jeans.

He looked too good. He was distracting her from the beauty that surrounded her. The shoreline slipped by, the dark brown and green of the spruce highlighted by the

52 LAKE OF DREAMS

white trunks of the birch trees. Gray rock thrust out from the trees, falling in broken steps to the water.

She looked ahead, searching for the particular configuration of trees she knew marked the mouth of the Maribel River. There it was, the two tall pine trees next to the one shaped sort of like a face with a big nose. She turned the canoe on a course straight for them.

The air was still with the approaching twilight. They were paddling parallel to the shore, about forty feet out. Birdcalls sounded from the forest lining the shore. Then Michael spotted something moving through the water between the canoe and the shore. "What on earth is that?" he said over his shoulder.

Pema looked to where he pointed and saw the line of disturbance where something had just passed through the water. Moving her eyes ahead, she spotted the mysterious swimmer. In front it had a small brown lump. About three feet back from that, some bright green things were sticking up into the air, flapping.

"I have no idea." This was part of the lure of the bush for her, the chance to experience something new and unknown. "Let's try to get closer."

"Maybe it's the big wave you were telling me about earlier," said Michael. He continued to paddle with long, even strokes, and Pema turned the canoe so they would intercept the object. "It's trying to lure us closer so it can eat our canoe."

"It's got the wrong lake. We don't get to Big Wave until tomorrow."

"Okay, it's the Breton Monster. Related to the Loch Ness Monster. We'll go down in history as being the ones to discover and tame it. I can see it, we'll go on a world tour. You can wear a spangled bikini and I'll have a top hat and tails. The world will beat a path to our door,

LAKE OF DREAMS 53

begging to pay us so they can see the monster. We'll call it Lenny.''

Pema grinned. What an imagination! She felt a warm glow at the thought that Michael seemed to be enjoying the challenge of a new experience as much as she did. ''Those green things in the back look a lot like leaves. And the lump in front, do you think it's a bump on a log?''

''A self-propelling log?''

''It can't be. There must be something under it, pushing it.''

''Maybe the green in the back is its feet or tail or something and the lump in front is its head.''

''Green feet?'' Pema smiled.

''A new species, never before known to man. Or woman.''

As they approached the moving thing, it began to speed up. The green part bobbed up and down in the water as it moved along. They moved closer. Then suddenly the brown lump moved ahead of the green part. As it dove under the water, a wide, flat object appeared and slapped the surface with a smack. Michael jumped, startled. Pema began to laugh.

''Look.'' She pointed to where a tree branch floated by itself in the water, a few leaves still clinging to one end. ''It was a beaver. It was pulling that branch. So much for your new scientific discoveries.''

Michael laughed, too. He rested his paddle across the bow of the canoe and looked at Pema. She was searching the surface of the water for any sign of the beaver. ''That's what I like so much about being up here,'' she said. ''There's always something new to learn. It teaches you to look at the world in a different way, sort of like a child seeing everything for the first time.''

54 LAKE OF DREAMS

Michael picked up his paddle and began a stroke. From behind him, he heard Pema begin to sing.

My paddle's keen and bright
Flashing with silver
Quick as the wild goose flies
Dip, dip and swing
Dip, dip and swing her back
Flashing with silver
Follow the wild goose trail
Dip, dip and swing.

The sun was nearing the horizon, and soft pink and orange streaks extended out from behind a necklace of clouds that ran along the edge of the sky. Michael breathed in deeply and felt the fresh, clean air pass into every part of his lungs. He dug his paddle into the water, pulled it back and lifted and swung it forward. His body moved easily in the rhythm, his muscles working. He listened to Pema's clear, sweet voice and realized that he felt really good.

Pema brought the canoe alongside a rock shelf. "Our campsite," she said.

Michael looked around as he scrambled onto dry land. The rock led to a small clearing. The ground was fairly flat, covered with moss. Trees surrounded the clear area.

"The bugs will be out in force soon," said Pema as she tied the canoe at both ends. "We'd better get into long-sleeved shirts. Then we'll get the tents up."

A short while later she glanced over to where Michael stood looking dubiously at his sagging tent. It was made of blue fabric and was really two tents, an inner one covered by an outer fly with an airspace between the two

LAKE OF DREAMS 55

layers. She suspected that he had never been in a tent before, much less had to put one up.

"We'll have a quick meal tonight." Coming up to Michael's tent, she fiddled with a rope and pushed on a couple of the pegs. The tent stood up straight. "I never cook the first night out. There's bread, cold meat and cheese."

"I just want to wash up." Michael got his soap from his pack and headed to the lake, when he found Pema standing in front of him.

"Here," she said, handing him a big plastic tub. "Fill it with water, and when you're done, carry the soapy water into the bush and pour it out."

"Why?" He was confused. "Surely the little bit of soap I'll use won't even be noticed in that huge lake."

"Wrong. I know I sound like a fanatic, but this is important. The lapping action of the waves on the shore can build up a lot of soap bubbles. If everyone put just a tiny bit of soap in the water, it would add up to a soapy, dead lake. You city people—"

"Whoa, whoa." Michael held the tub up as a shield. "Please, I may be an ignorant yuppie, but I'm willing to learn."

She sighed. What could she do? "All right, but remember one thing. When we leave this campsite tomorrow, it should look exactly as it does now. No one should be able to tell that there was anyone here."

"Sounds exciting." He passed her after having filled up the tub with water from the lake. "Are we being chased? Is a gang of international spies on our tail? We must remain hidden and cover all signs of our trail. Are you carrying secret documents? Or is it jewels that you're smuggling out of the country?"

56   LAKE OF DREAMS

''We're not near any borders,'' said Pema dryly, but she was smiling.

The long twilight, a time of soft light and hushed sounds from birds and insects, had ended. Michael lay in his tent. At first he had the feeling that his ears were blocked, but soon he realized it was simply because it was so silent out here. There were occasional scurrying and rustling noises, and he could hear the water lapping at the shore, but that was it. Under it all was a silence as soft and rich as velvet.

He was proud of himself. He had spent two hours in a canoe and it hadn't been all that bad. It had been fun in a way, it had filled a part of himself he hadn't even known was empty. Or maybe he had. He thought of the urge that had brought him here, to this isolated lakeshore in northern Saskatchewan. He had wanted to get away from the city. He had wanted to be able to do some of his work in a natural setting. He still didn't understand why he had this urge, but he was starting to feel how right it was.

He wriggled his body in his sleeping bag. This wasn't as uncomfortable as he'd feared. The thin foam pad under the bag made a pretty good bed. He did miss his radio, though. He'd always liked to listen to the late news report before going to bed. He was completely cut off from the world he knew. Anything could be happening—a stock market crash in New York, an earthquake leveling Toronto, a flying saucer kidnapping the queen of England—and he wouldn't know. A larger rustling sound passed by pretty close to his tent. A bear? Michael wondered if Pema was in her green tent next to his, or if she had crept off and stranded him here. ''Pema?''

''Yes?'' he heard out of the darkness.

LAKE OF DREAMS 57

Michael realized he couldn't tell her he had been wondering if she was still there. He had to think of something to say. "When I asked you about your dreams, you told me about graduate school. I don't want to be nosy, but I was wondering how the lake is tied up with your going to university."

Pema had been lying in her tent remembering when she and Michael had seen the mysterious swimming object. It had been fun, and she knew it had been an even more memorable experience because Michael had been there with her. Maybe it was because of the shared laughter then, or because of the anonymous enclosing darkness, but she answered him frankly.

"Meniskamee is part of the dream. I've been corresponding with this professor of biology, Dr. Hathaway. He wants me to come and work with him. We've discussed the research I could do. I would do fieldwork here and then take my data to him and we'd work together on it."

"And how does the lake fit in?" Michael's voice was gentle in the night.

"The lake is the research. It's a pretty independent ecosystem. The plants and animals fit together so well. Each life form has its separate place, and yet each is dependent on the others.

"I want to study them. I want to know how they do it, live together so well. There is violence, of course, some of them are prey and others are hunters. But they respect each other, they know that all are needed for the whole. There's a balance. I can't help feeling that if I can learn how they do it, how the small number of species that live in and around Meniskamee can form a harmonious system, then maybe I can learn how a larger number of species can do it. Maybe I can even learn how man could fit into the world in the same way.''

Pema fell silent. She looked at the slanting green walls that enclosed her. She had never talked about her hopes to anyone except Dr. Hathaway. Her brothers knew that the lake was tied up with her plans for graduate school, but when she tried to tell them of her visions of all beings living together respecting their mutual needs, the way it was at Meniskamee, they smiled fondly at her, but she knew they didn't understand.

She sighed. If she did go back to school, she could take agricultural courses. Maybe she would learn something that could help her brothers in their farming, and make it better for the land, too. But she hadn't gone back to school yet. She was still saving money, even though she knew she had enough. Dr. Hathaway had told her he could pay her a small salary from his research grant. Some of it was always allocated to help promising students.

Michael's voice came to her. ''Your research project sounds like it would be very worthwhile. Why haven't you begun?''

Pema closed her eyes. That was the question. Why hadn't she begun? Last winter, she had actually sent in an application to the University of Toronto. When she'd received the letter of acceptance, she'd stood, holding it in her hand, for a long time. Then she had stuck it in the back of her desk drawer. It was still there.

She had last talked to Dr. Hathaway only a couple of weeks earlier. He wanted to know if she was coming. She had said she would think about it. And she knew that was all she would do.

How could she explain to anyone the fear she had? She thought back to when she had been taking courses

LAKE OF DREAMS

for the Bachelor of Education degree. She had had to work very hard to get her good marks. The other students had spent a lot of time talking together and sitting and drinking in the university pub. They had gone to parties and dances. They had worn stylish clothes and had modern haircuts. Pema had felt she didn't belong, that she shouldn't really be there. There were other rural students there, too, people who had grown up on farms as she had, but she didn't fit in with them, either. When she talked to them about her canoe and her Métis grandfather, they listened but they didn't hear.

It was only when she was doing the practical part of her degree, when she was in the classroom teaching, that she had felt she belonged. The kids liked her, and she could communicate with them. She told them things, and they understood. And the teachers watching and judging her were impressed.

Graduate school would be just like the course part of her education degree, she knew, only worse. The competition was tougher in a master's program. The students were better, smarter. Pema knew that she was bright enough, but she needed to study really hard to do well. How could she hope to even hold her own, never mind compete, with the sorts of students she would find in her classes?

And she would have to leave Saskatoon, leave her family. Leave her brothers, leave the job she loved, leave her friends. She would have to move to Toronto, to the big city.

She realized Michael was waiting for an answer to his question. How could she tell him the answer, that she hadn't let her dream become reality because she was afraid? He shouldn't be asking her these questions. It

60 LAKE OF DREAMS

was none of his business. And what's more, if he had his way, her dream would become impossible anyway.

"I'm not going to graduate school because you want to buy my lake," she burst out. "Without Meniskamee I can't do the research. Somehow I doubt that when you have your executives there in their three-piece suits you'll want a biology student covered with mud poking around. I would ruin your corporate image."

She lay silently, then heard Michael get up and unzip his tent. She watched through the transparent end of her tent as he passed by on his way to the biffy, the hole in the ground she had dug at the edge of the clearing farthest from the lake. She could see in the moonlight that he was wearing only a pair of jeans.

Good, she thought, I hope every blackfly and mosquito in Saskatchewan takes a bite.

Michael returned to his tent, got into the sleeping bag and scratched. What sort of uncivilized place was this where a man couldn't even relieve himself without being eaten alive? Pema had given him some gunky insect repellent to use, but he'd washed it off before getting in his sleeping bag. There had probably been more mosquitos out there in that small patch of bush than there were in the whole city of Toronto. And their whining. It was enough to drive him crazy. Even here in the tent, he could still hear it.

What was with Pema to jump on him like that? Yesterday at the airport they had talked about dreams and they had been open and sharing. Tonight she had shut him out completely.

He sat up. That whining was very loud. Oh, no, it couldn't be. Some bug, not satisfied with what it had eaten of him outside, had followed him here, into his tent. He turned on his flashlight and began looking for the bug.

Of course, yesterday Pema hadn't known he was after her precious lake. Well, he was sorry if he might interfere with her plans, but she had obviously been meaning to do this research there for some time. What was stopping her? Was she one of those people who was all talk and no action? He hadn't thought so, but you never knew.

Ah, there was the bug. It was moving upward along the wall of the tent, bouncing off the material. He raised himself onto his knees and held his hand out, ready to strike. Whack! There, he got the little whiner. The tent trembled as he lay down. He rolled over in his bag, turning his back on the silence coming from the other tent, and went to sleep.

Pema woke very early the next morning. She picked up her jeans, underwear and a flannel shirt. Glancing over at Michael's tent, she saw no signs of movement, so she crept quickly down to the lake. The water was smooth and glassy in the early morning calm, and a mist was rising from the surface. Putting her clothes in the canoe, Pema walked into the water.

Michael sat up in his tent and rubbed the sleep from his eyes. He moved on hands and knees to the front and unzipped the doorway. He was just about to step outside and stretch when he heard a sound from the lake.

Pema stood knee-deep in the water, her back to him. She wasn't wearing anything. He drew in his breath at the sight of her long, slim body. Her mahogany hair streamed down her back almost to her hips, glinting gold where the rays of the rising sun caught it. She bent and scooped up some water in her hands, pouring it over her shoulders. His eyes followed the silvery stream as it ran down her body. Drops shining like diamonds caught in her hair, then cascaded from the ends of her hair onto the rounded firmness of her buttocks and ran down the lithe length of her legs. She leaned over at the waist, her knees bent and straightened, and she dove cleanly into the lake.

Michael waited until her sleek head appeared about thirty feet out. She began to swim with powerful strokes parallel to the shore. He went into his tent, his breathing ragged. She was so beautiful, a natural woman in a natural environment. She belonged here, with the water and the sky. Despite the differences in their outlooks on the world, despite the fact that she was opposed to his buying the lake, he wanted her. She was special, as he'd known from the moment he'd first seen her.

Pema came back from her swim feeling refreshed and ready for anything. The water had been cold but invigorating. She glanced up the shore at the blue tent. Still no sign of life. She pulled her clothes on and went to get her fishing rod. She might as well do something useful while she waited for him.

When she returned, Michael was sitting on the bank, his head hung back so his face was to the sun. He looked up as she approached.

"Here, catch," she called. Michael automatically put his hands out to catch the black object that she threw to him. The thing landed in his hands with a squelch. It felt cold and slimy. He dropped it quickly, then looked down to see what it was. It was a fish, a dead one.

"I did well," said Pema. She unloaded her fishing tackle. "Four fat trout. We'll have a good meal later. Aren't they lovely?"

LAKE OF DREAMS 63

"Beautiful," said Michael. He gingerly picked up the trout lying at his feet. It was covered with dirt, so he took it down to the lake to rinse.

She handed him a knife and a bucket with the three other fish. "Why don't you clean these while I wash out the canoe. Then we'll eat breakfast."

Clean them? What did clean fish mean? He examined the one in his hand. He had just rinsed it, so it couldn't be dirty. He looked up to find her grinning at him.

"Lay the fish on a rock," she said. "Hold its tail and run the knife from the vent up the belly to its head. Tilt the knife blade like this." She demonstrated as she spoke. "There." She left fish and knife on the ground and stood up. "Any problem?"

"No, of course not." He sat on a rock that stuck out into the water and looked at the fish she had cut open.

Her grin widened. "Now disembowel it." It would be good for him to learn that fish weren't swimming around in the lakes of the world with no heads and their insides stuffed with shrimp and aromatic herbs. She carried her gear up to the camp.

When she finished rinsing out the canoe, Pema went over to Michael. Fish guts were everywhere. They coated the skin of his hands, they stuck to his clothes. He even had some smudged on his face. The smell of fish was also everywhere. But he had done an admirable job of cleaning three of the trout and was almost done with the fourth.

Michael put the last fish in the collapsible bucket with the others. Laying the knife down, he stood up and tried to brush off his clothes. When that didn't work, he waded into the lake, clothes and all.

64 LAKE OF DREAMS

Pema watched as he ducked under the water and began to rinse his hair. Smiling, she picked up the knife and the bucket. A shout came to her from the lake.

"Here, catch."

His shirt landed with a wet plop on the rock beside her. She looked out to where he stood hip deep in the water. He was stepping out of his jeans. She stared at his wet skin glistening in the sunlight, at the mat of dark hair plastered to his broad chest. Her eyes followed the hair as it narrowed, forming a dark line that extended below his stomach before disappearing beneath the water. His jeans, crumpled into a wet ball, landed next to his shirt.

"Would you wring those out for me?" he called.

She still stared. His hips were narrow, his stomach flat, layered with muscle. He took a step into shallower water. She swallowed and quickly ducked her head, picking up his jeans. She heard him laugh as she began twisting the denim, squeezing out the water. Then a splash told her that he had dived.

Without looking at the lake, Pema spread Michael's clothes on the canoe to dry. She put the fish in a plastic bag and put the bag in a bucket of cool water. Only then did she allow her eyes to search out Michael.

He was swimming with powerful strokes in from the center of the lake. It was on the tip of her tongue to call out to him. Didn't he know you should always swim along the shore, so if you had problems you were never too far out? But the words died as she saw how beautifully he swam. His arms cut cleanly through the water, each stroke propelling him with grace and strength. His legs kicked rhythmically, his arms rose and fell, water droplets flying from them in a silver spray.

To Pema, he looked like some ancient water creature, a god, perhaps, a man who belonged in the water, who

LAKE OF DREAMS 65

was one with it. She wanted to stay and watch as he emerged, water dripping from his hair, running in streams down his skin, but as he began walking toward her she remembered that he was nude, and she turned and began walking up to the tents.

"Why don't you come in and swim with me?" he called.

She stopped walking but did not turn around.

"Come on," he continued, "I know you like swimming, too."

She felt a hot flush stain her cheeks. He had seen her, he must have, when she had swum early this morning.

"Come join me," he called again.

Pema wanted to. She wanted to join him, to swim with him, both of them in their natural state, both of them one with the water and the sky. She turned slowly to face him. He stood, again hip deep. Her hand went to the top button of her flannel shirt.

She knew he wanted to see her remove her clothes and come to him. She knew she wanted to do it. She wanted to walk down the bank, her body held tall and proud, for him. She wanted to walk through the water, feeling it move up her legs, over her hips, until she stood before him. She would raise her arms, put her hands on his shoulders, trail her fingers over his wet skin, down over the wet hair that covered his chest. She would . . .

No. She would not. He would see it as her giving herself to him. He wanted her, she knew, but he also wanted that other part of her, Meniskamee. If he got the part of her that she wanted to give, would he not think he could have all? No, he would have nothing. So she turned toward the tents again, calling, "No, thanks, I swam already. I'll start breakfast." And she ignored the voice inside of her that sang a song of loss.

Chapter Four

Pema decided to save the fish for lunch, and set out oatmeal, nuts and dried fruit for breakfast. She boiled water for the oatmeal, but when it came time to pour the oats into the pot, she found herself staring into the swirling bubbles in the water, the bag of oatmeal hanging from her hand. She didn't feel like cooking. She didn't even feel like eating.

Her stomach was unsettled, and she knew tension was the reason. Part of it was because she had wanted to swim with Michael. But she couldn't act as if everything was wonderful between them when it wasn't. She mustn't let herself forget the reason he was here. Swimming together like that was something lovers did. Their relationship, whatever it was, was definitely not a loving one.

But standing there, staring at the boiling water in the pot, Pema realized that she was upset over more than the swimming incident. It was the conversation last night,

LAKE OF DREAMS

when she had talked about why she hadn't gone to graduate school.

She didn't like thinking about that, much less talking about it. Most of the time she was able to convince herself that the reasons she hadn't gone yet were good ones. Money was important, wasn't it? And leaving behind one's family was a big step. She would still go someday, wouldn't she? But last night, and still this morning, she was forced to admit something to herself. The reasons she used were not good ones at all. The only reason she wasn't following her dream was that she was afraid.

And now Michael knew, too. Why had she told him? Did he now think of her as a weak person? Well, if he did, he was wrong. She had to prove that he was wrong. She had strength, she knew it. She had simply never tested herself. It was time she did.

She dumped the oatmeal in the pot. "Here's your breakfast," she called to him. "You'd better stir it so it doesn't stick." She disappeared into her tent.

"My breakfast?" Michael said. He had finished his swim and was dressed in shorts and a T-shirt. "What about yours?"

Pema came out, wearing her bathing suit. "I'm not hungry."

He followed her down to the lake. "What are you doing?"

"I'm going to swim across the lake."

"What? Now?" He squinted across the sun-flecked water. "It must be at least two miles."

"What's the matter? Don't you think I can do it?" She turned to face him.

"I don't know if you can do it," he said. "I don't know enough about your swimming abilities. But I do know that even the most experienced swimmer wouldn't go out without having eaten anything and without a boat along for safety.''

"This is something I have to do." Pema waded a few steps into the water. "I have to prove something to myself. And to you."

"You don't have to prove—" Michael began, but with a splash she dove into the water. He watched her swimming for a moment, her arms flashing gold in the sun. Then he headed for the canoe.

He put two paddles and life jackets in the boat. Just as he was about to get in, he glanced back at the fire and the pot of oatmeal bubbling merrily. He ran up to it and, using a stick, pulled the pot off the fire and set it on the ground. Then he jumped into the canoe and paddled after Pema.

She was quite a way out, and all he could see was the round, dark bump that was her head and the circular motions of her arms. It took him a few minutes to adjust to paddling the canoe by himself. With just his weight in it, even though he was kneeling, it rode higher in the water, and so was more at the mercy of the wind. On the other hand, the canoe was more sensitive to what he did with the paddle, and was more maneuverable.

He was forced to spend some time experimenting with what was the best way to get the canoe to go in a straight line, and during that time Pema moved farther out into the center of the lake. He moved closer to the side of the canoe, so that it tipped slightly, but felt how quickly it responded to his paddle. Feeling in control, hearing the sound of the water rushing by beneath his knees, he followed her.

Pema's body felt good. Her muscles were working well, arms circling and pulling, legs kicking. The water was cool against her heated skin. She thought that maybe she was swimming too fast; after all, there was a lot of lake left to cross. But she wanted to work hard, she wanted to push herself to her limit. If she didn't try, how could she know what she was capable of? She had to try, had to prove to Michael that...

Her breathing was coming harder now, and she switched to breast stroke. Was she doing this to prove something to Michael or to herself? It's for myself, she thought fiercely. What he thinks of me doesn't matter. I can't let it matter. She started doing the crawl again, welcoming the feeling of her muscles working, straining to pull her through the water. A welcome numbness spread through her mind, dulling the thoughts about Michael and whether he thought her weak because she hadn't gone after her dream.

Without warning, the cramp struck. It took hold of her at her waist, squeezing and twisting. She tried to drownproof, floating facedown so she could massage the stricken muscle, but the pain was too great. She lifted her head to get a breath, but the surface was suddenly far away, above her.

And then she felt a strong arm around her chest. It was tight, like a band of steel, and for a moment she fought it, imagining it was the tentacle of some monster trying to drag her down to its watery lair. But the arm was too strong, and it wouldn't let go, and then her face broke the surface and she gasped in a long, shuddering gulp of air. "It's okay," she heard a voice say. "Relax, I've got you. You're okay."

Pema stopped struggling. The water, which had seemed an enemy only moments before, supported her now.

"That's my girl," she heard. The voice was soothing, and she felt it envelop her in warmth. Her breathing slowed, and the pain of the cramp lessened. She became aware that her head was resting on a strong, broad shoulder and that the arm was still tight around her. After a few moments she was able to lift her head and look around. Michael was close behind her, his arm holding her up in the water.

"Where did you come from?" she asked.

"That's it?" he said. "Those are your words to your rescuer? No 'My hero! Oh, how can I ever repay you?'" He grinned at her, his hair, even darker from the water, falling into his eyes.

She smiled back and realized how hard he was working to tread water while he supported her. She rubbed at her abdomen, massaging the last of the cramp away. She moved away from him a bit, and found that she could tread water on her own. "How did you get here?" she asked.

"By canoe." Michael watched her carefully to make sure she was okay.

She looked around. "What canoe?"

He looked over his shoulder. There was a canoe shape in the water, but it was far away, and drifting farther each second. "Oh, no," he groaned. "I didn't think about the wind. When I saw you in trouble, I dove in the water and . . . Well, all I could think of was you."

"I'm glad you did. Thank you," Pema said softly. "You were right and I was wrong. I shouldn't have tried to swim alone. But I wanted to try so bad, I wanted—" She felt tears begin to burn behind her eyelids.

"Hush," said Michael. "You could have done it. You're a strong swimmer, I know that now. You can do anything you try, you know."

LAKE OF DREAMS

She shook her head and forced back the tears. "It was stupid. I was swimming too fast and I got the cramp. If only I'd been sensible and not pushed myself so hard."

"It's okay to fail," he said. "At least it means you're trying. And you can always try again."

Pema looked at him. His broad shoulders were above the lake surface, and she could see the muscles in them rippling with the exertion of treading water. His hair was plastered tight to his head, making him look older and harder somehow. He reached out and pushed her hair, heavy with water, from her face. She closed her eyes, reveling in the feeling of his skin warm against hers, and knew that he had done much more for her than merely rescuing her from drowning.

His hand left the side of her head and she opened her eyes. "Perhaps," he said, "it would be a good idea to chase the canoe."

She gasped. The near-drowning had obviously affected her brain. Here they were in the middle of a lake, and their transportation to shore was drifting away. She started to swim after the canoe.

"Wait," Michael said. "I don't think you should be swimming yet. Wait here and I'll go get it."

"I'm fine." Pema felt her voice grow tight. He did think she was weak. "Come on, I'll race you."

"No." He grabbed the back of her bathing suit.

She pulled free of his grasp. "Okay, think of it this way. If I'm going to get in trouble again, which I'm not, mind you, wouldn't it be better if I was swimming beside you rather than left here all alone?"

Michael shook his head ruefully. "Your logic leaves me speechless. Come on, then. But we will swim slowly."

"We'd better swim faster than the wind or we'll have an awfully long swim."

72 LAKE OF DREAMS

He laughed and they set off together.

In the end, fifteen minutes of fairly fast swimming was necessary for them to catch up to the canoe. Pema paced herself carefully at first, afraid that the cramp might recur, but her body responded well to the demands of swimming and she felt no pain. By the time they reached the canoe, though, both she and Michael were breathing hard.

He grabbed the gunwale with one hand. "Boy," he said. "I don't know if I can drag myself up into the boat."

Pema swam to the stern and hung on to the end, hooking her feet on the gunwales on each side. She relaxed, feeling the canoe bob gently and the water lapping at her skin. Then suddenly she bolted upright in the water. "Come on, we've got to get back to shore as quickly as possible."

Michael looked at her in surprise, but he pulled himself over the side of the canoe and then held it steady while she climbed in. She picked up a paddle.

"What's the hurry?" he asked.

"The oatmeal." Pema was paddling hard. "It's probably too late. It'll be one solid burned mess, and we won't have a cooking pot."

He began to laugh.

She sent him a dark look. "You may laugh now, but it won't seem so funny when we can't cook anything."

"It's okay," he said. "I took the pot off the fire before I came after you."

She stopped paddling and rested her paddle across the gunwales. "This is really your day, isn't it. You not only rescue me, you rescue my cooking pot, too. Still, I'm glad you had your priorities straight. Food first, then me."

LAKE OF DREAMS 73

"It's been my pleasure." Michael pretended to sweep a hat off his head and made a deep bow from where he was kneeling in the canoe. "I'll think of a suitable way you can reward me, later."

Pema smiled, but she knew the smile didn't reach her eyes. Michael had saved her from two possible bad consequences of her foolishness. He had told her that failure didn't matter, as long as you tried to go after your dream. She started paddling again. He seemed so sure of himself, so competent. Had he ever failed at something? And did he think of her as weak?

"We're coming to the portage," Pema said. The canoe was moving smoothly through the water. They had eaten their breakfast. The oatmeal had cooked by itself during the time it spent sitting in the hot water. It was only lukewarm, but it tasted good after all their excitement. After eating, she and Michael had set out along the Maribel River. "We need to get from here over to Big Wave Lake. After that, I think I'll show you how to paddle stern. I'll need to teach you J-stroke. If Big Wave is windy, we'll be better off with your weight in the stern."

"Sounds good," said Michael. "You know me, I like to be in control."

"Do I?" She paused in her paddling to tuck a stray strand of hair behind her ear. "Know you, I mean?"

"You know me."

Pema said nothing. She wasn't sure she knew him at all. Who was he? The friendly, attractive stranger at the airport? The big-city successful businessman? Or the silent-footed predator she had sensed lurking behind his eyes?

74   LAKE OF DREAMS

"But," he continued, "I'll fill you in on some details, if you'd like."

"Yes." She was eager to talk about something neutral. "Tell me about your family."

"My family. My father is a stockbroker and my mother is a lawyer. I'm the only child. My father wanted me to follow in his firm, so I went to the University of Western Ontario, to the business school. But I didn't like dealing in stocks. I liked computers. I left Christie and Korbett and got a job with a big computer firm. And then later I started my own company."

"Did your father mind?"

"Probably. But he and my mother have always been very supportive. As long as I'm living up to my potential, they will agree with what I want to do."

"Did your mother work even when you were very little?"

"Yes. There was always a nanny in the house. But my parents loved me, I knew that. They made sure we had some time together every day, quality time. I was a happy child."

"I was a happy child, too," said Pema. "My brothers raised me. They surrounded me with love. They were busy, of course, running the farm, but I was always included in everything they did. I sat in the tractors with them. I helped milk the few cows we kept. I was in charge of the chickens when I was five years old."

She paused, staring across the lake. The surface of the water danced and sparkled in the sunlight. "My brothers called me Princess," she continued. Her voice was low, and Michael needed to turn his head over his shoulder to hear. "They made me crowns of wildflowers to wear. I always knew I was special. But somehow, I knew I was different, too."

LAKE OF DREAMS 75

She fell silent again. "Different in what way?" Michael asked.

"Oh, because I was a girl. I figured out pretty early that there was a world they lived in that I couldn't enter, could never be a part of. They were my whole family, my brothers, and I was cut off from them. But when I was little, it didn't matter, because they made me feel as if my world was such a wondrous place that I was lucky to be there."

"I don't understand." He stopped paddling and twisted in his seat.

"I was female. I was special, but I was also delicate, weaker. I couldn't be exposed to their hard, physical world. I needed to be petted, protected."

"Sounds like chauvinism to me," said Michael. "In my family, people are judged by their merits, not by their sex. Look at my mother. She made it, all on her own, in a tough, traditionally male profession."

Pema was paddling by herself, with short, choppy strokes. "Yes, but what did she give up? She was so busy trying to make it in a man's world, she was too busy to take part in her own world. She was too busy for you. Women are different in some ways. Women are mothers. I don't believe that a woman is liberated just because she can act like a man. A liberated woman is one who has a choice to be whoever she wants to be."

Michael turned and began paddling again.

"My brothers were wonderful at raising me," Pema continued. "One thing they knew, even though they were men, was how to show love. They hugged me, and laughed with me. But I'm not like you. Do you always succeed in everything you do?"

"What?" Michael was startled by this sudden change of topic.

"You seem so sure of yourself," she said. "You're at the top in your profession, owning your own company. You're good-looking, you're a good swimmer, you learn things easily, like canoeing."

"I'm speechless. And I'm flattered you have such a high opinion of me." Michael stopped speaking, realizing his words sounded sarcastic. He was a little embarrassed by what she had said, and sarcasm was one way to handle it. But more lay beneath the surface of her words than was immediately apparent. He took a moment to think about how he should respond.

"I really am flattered that this is how you perceive me," he said. "I guess I have achieved a certain level of success in some areas. But it hasn't come easily. I've had to work very hard to get where I am."

"But weren't you ever afraid of failing?" she asked.

Michael could hear how her words hummed with intensity. "Of course I was," he said. "And sometimes I did fail. Look at my illustrious hockey career, for example. And my attempts to go into business with my father."

"You seem so sure of yourself," Pema said.

"Perhaps that sort of confidence comes from knowing I've done my best. In hockey, I had to admit finally that I just wasn't good enough. It wasn't easy. I'd done my best and it wasn't enough. But at least I'd tried. And once I'd adjusted to the fact that I wasn't going to be a hockey star, making millions and having women swooning every time I smiled at them, I tried something else. Eventually I found the work I do now, which I love, and which I am good enough to do."

Pema felt the skin of her hands rubbing against the smooth surface of the paddle. Her hands were always

LAKE OF DREAMS 77

tender during the first trip each season, until the calluses had time to form.

"You also are successful," she heard Michael say. "You are very attractive, and you move with grace and confidence. Out here, in the bush, you know what you're doing. You're good at it, you know it, and it shows. Out here, I'm the one who is uncertain and afraid."

She almost laughed at the thought of him being afraid of anything. He was big and strong, and he was willing, eager almost, to try new things. That was one of the things she liked about him, in fact.

She thought about what he'd said. It was easy to be confident when you were in your own environment. His was the city and hers was out here, each had a place where they knew they were capable. But canoeing hadn't always been so familiar to her. She'd had to learn it once; she'd had to try and perhaps fail. Getting her teaching degree hadn't been easy but she'd done it. Perhaps going to graduate school was something she could try.

"You realize," Michael said, "that we've both just admitted we find each other attractive?"

Pema nodded, then realized he couldn't see her. She looked at his broad back and smiled. "So we did. But don't you get too conceited."

"I won't," he said. "It's enough, for now."

For now? What did that mean? Pema wished she could see his face, but had to content herself with watching the back of his head. She liked the way his dark hair caught the sunlight, reflecting it in reddish glints.

They paddled in silence for a while. Actually, Pema wasn't silent all the time, even though she wasn't speaking. She sang, little songs with soaring melodies, songs

78   LAKE OF DREAMS

that spoke of wind and water, of being alone but not lonely, of freedom.

The day was very warm, the air still. The lake water was calm, and the bow of the canoe cut through it with hardly a ripple. The sun was hot across her shoulders. She breathed in the scent of the lake, a mixture of water, fish, green things, a smell of life.

The sound of the water lapping at the bow was like a counterpoint to her music. The water sang in harmony with her.

Pema turned the canoe in at a small, muddy bank. "This is the start of the portage." She maneuvered the canoe until it was parallel to the bank, and stepped into the shallow water.

Michael got out, too, and held the canoe while she took first one and then the other pack out and put them on the shore. He helped her carry the canoe up the steep, muddy bank.

She handed him the paddles and life jackets. "Here, you can carry these as well as your pack." She picked up her pack and slipped the straps over her shoulders.

She then went to the canoe. Standing beside it in the middle, she pulled it until the hull rested on her thighs. Reaching across with one hand, she gripped the gunwale and slipped her other arm under the hull. Straightening her legs, she lifted with her arms, rolling the canoe onto her shoulders. She planted her feet firmly until she had the canoe balanced, then took the first steps onto the portage trail.

She looked at Michael, who was staring at her in amazement. "The canoe isn't very heavy," she said, grinning. "It's only sixty pounds. You can carry it on the next portage. This trail's fairly long. Three-quarters of

LAKE OF DREAMS 79

a mile. Let me know if you need a rest." She started walking.

She moved along the trail, her footfalls soft on the dirt. Her eyes scanned the path ahead of her, looking for roots that could trip her, for overhanging tree limbs that could catch the canoe. She liked portaging, liked the feeling of her canoe pressing on her shoulders. Her arms were outstretched in front of her, hands holding the gunwales, keeping the canoe balanced. What she had told Michael was true, it really wasn't hard carrying a canoe this way. Her shoulders and back were strong; her large frame was sturdy. The canoe wasn't a burden, but a friend.

"She ain't heavy, she's my canoe," she sang.

Walking behind her, Michael heard the song and smiled. "Do you know," he said, "that you look like a brown banana with legs?"

She laughed. "When we get to the end of the portage, I'll take my peel off."

"I'd like that," he said. His voice was low and rough.

"I meant the canoe."

"I know. But that's not what I meant."

To her surprise, Pema felt herself blush. Although she couldn't see him, Michael's voice was so intimate, his words almost a breathy whisper, that she could feel his green eyes warm against her body. She walked without seeing for a moment, and almost tripped over a stone in the trail.

"Look," said Michael. "There's something under that rock."

She stopped and turned to look. By the side of the trail, an old tea pail had been stashed under a rock. "Leave it," she said, as Michael went over to it. "It's probably been left by a trapper. He'll be back for it someday, either with his canoe, or on snowshoes, and he'll expect to find it where he left it."

"Really?" Michael was amazed at the thought of an object, left somewhere, not getting stolen.

"The bush is not like the city," Pema said. "People trust one another here. It's a matter of survival. That pail may contain a cache of food for that trapper. He can come here in the middle of winter and know that he'll find food. And no one will take it, because if they do, he'll die."

"I like that," Michael said. "Out here, in a harsher environment, people pull together. But the city environment is harsh, too."

"People in the city think only of themselves, though."

"Maybe," he continued, "people steal in the city because it's so obvious that some people have more than others. Out here, everyone is really in the same boat."

"Good pun," Pema interjected.

He groaned. "Pun unintended. But out here, no one is a lot richer than anyone else. You're all traveling through wild country, with little more than your canoes and tents."

"I understand," she said. "You're right, we're all people stripped down to bare necessities. No one can take from someone else without depriving him of something essential. We're all linked." She stopped speaking, but her thoughts continued in her head. Some people *are* richer. Right now, I feel rich, being here with you. Her eyes widened as the import of her thought took root. His presence here, having him to share things with, had added something to the trip. Something good.

At the end of the portage trail, Pema rolled the canoe off her shoulders and took off her pack. Rotating her shoulders a few times, she stared across Big Wave Lake.

LAKE OF DREAMS   81

It was a big lake, the far shore a hazy line in the distance. Michael came up beside her and put his pack down.

"Do you want to learn to stern?" she asked him.

He smiled at her. "I'd like that."

She looked into his face and felt her mouth stretch into a smile. "Your hair is all curly." She touched his hair, her fingers tangling themselves in his thick black curls.

"My hair always curls unless I brush it straight when it's wet." He reached up and trapped her hand beneath his. Slowly their joined hands were lowered, until they were there, a link, between their two bodies.

Pema looked at the hands. Michael moved his fingers until they were intertwined with hers. Then he put his other hand beneath her chin and tipped her face up to his.

The kiss was soft and very sweet. Only their mouths and their hands touched. His lips moved on hers, lightly at first, then with increasing pressure. And then their arms were around one another, their bodies pressed together.

The water lapped at the shore, its murmur a rhythmic song. A small wind blew, rustling the leaves of the trees, picking up a loose tendril of Pema's hair. Michael lifted his head and laughed as the long red tress was whipped across his face. She moved her head back, pulling her hair away from his eyes. She kept her hands linked around his neck.

"We should move on," she whispered.

"Okay, what's the next step? This?" He nuzzled her neck. "Or is it this?" And one hand slid up her back and over her shoulder to where it rested on one of her high, firm breasts.

Pema closed her eyes at the rush of sensation that fled outward from her breast to all parts of her body. His thumb brushed her nipple, which stood up, thrusting against the material of her shirt.

"No," she said, "no." But she could feel the way her breast fit so neatly into his cupped hand, as if it was made for him. It was wrong, though, the heat and excitement were wrong. She couldn't let herself get close to this man. Not now, not ever. She took a quick step backward, and her heel hit a tree root. She tripped and sat down a little too quickly.

Michael looked at her sitting on the ground. Her hair had come loose from the clip that held it, her cheeks were flushed, her eyes a darker green. He extended a hand to help her up.

Pema was suddenly afraid of any contact with him. She stood, pushing on the ground with both hands, and then turned to the food pack. "I think we should have a snack," she said. She held out a bag of trail mix—a mixture of nuts, raisins and chocolate chips. "It's high energy," she explained.

"I feel quite energized, thank you," he said.

His eyes were locked on hers and she couldn't look away. She held her breath.

He reached a hand toward her, and she thought he was going to brush her cheek. But he only took a handful of the trail mix from the bag she held, and turned to face the lake.

She tied up the bag and put it in the pack, not knowing whether to be relieved or sorry he hadn't touched her. She needed time, time to sort out her feelings for this man. She didn't know, though, how much time he would give her.

LAKE OF DREAMS

83

They got in the canoe, facing each other, the gear left on the shore, and Pema explained how to steer a canoe. "The stern paddler is always more powerful. Not just because of strength, but because the stroke is taken closer to the end of the canoe, and so has more leverage. A straight paddle stroke will, as well as moving the canoe forward, always have the effect of turning the canoe slightly in the opposite direction to the side the paddle is on. And so if both paddlers just take straight strokes, the canoe will slowly turn toward the opposite side to the stern paddler's side. You need to compensate."

"I understand," Michael said. "This morning, when I was paddling alone, I kept having to change sides until I figured out a kind of sideways stroke..." He stopped speaking, not sure if she wanted to be reminded of why he had been out alone in the canoe. She didn't say anything, though, and he couldn't tell what she was thinking.

She showed him the J-stroke, in which, after the straight stroke, the paddle is turned and pushed slightly outward from the side of the canoe. Michael tried it and felt how this little hook pushed the canoe back toward his paddling side. By adjusting how hard and far he pushed the paddle sideways, he could keep the canoe on a straight course.

As during the first lesson, Pema was surprised and pleased by how quickly Michael learned what she showed him. "You seem to have a real feel for a canoe," she said.

"Thank you," he said. "You know, that's one of the things I like about you."

She looked at him inquisitively.

"You're free with compliments," he continued. "I know I'm not exactly your favorite person right now, but if you think I'm doing something well, like learning to canoe, you say so. I appreciate that."

Pema felt herself start to blush, and turned her head so he wouldn't see. He was open about his feelings, too. "Why don't you take us back to shore?" she said quickly.

He was right, he wasn't one of her favorite people. He couldn't be, not if he was going to buy her lake. So why did hearing what he had just said send a warm glow through her skin?

Back on shore, she started a fire and got out the bag of fish. Michael watched as she fried them lightly in a little oil and garnished them with dried parsley from a small waterproof container.

He looked at the fish, steaming gently on his plate, took a bite and sighed with satisfaction. "This is better than any fish I've had at the best restaurants in Toronto."

"Everything tastes better here," she said. "In part, it's because it's fresh."

"True," he agreed. "Fish doesn't come much fresher than this."

"But it's also," she continued, "because you're eating it outdoors, after a hard morning's paddling."

"And don't forget the ambience of this restaurant." He swept his arm so it encompassed the lake surrounded by trees. "And the view. How could food not taste good when it's eaten here?"

She served him some more of the noodles she'd cooked to accompany the fish. "I'm surprised to hear you say that. I'd have thought that, to you, a meal

LAKE OF DREAMS

wouldn't be complete without linen tablecloths, crystal glasses and expensive wine to go in them."

Michael looked at her with a hurt expression. "Hey, I'm open to new experiences. That's one of the things, in fact, I like about the city. There is such a variety of people and places there. This trip is another chance for me to try something new.'

"It's a learning experience, eh?" She began to gather up the dishes. "Grit your teeth and bear it, you're going to learn something, or else?"

"That may be how I regarded it at the beginning." His gaze was intent on her face, and she felt herself held by the green of his eyes. "But," he continued, "I'm beginning to change my mind."

She sat without moving, her eyes still held by his. Change his mind? About what? Could it be that he was beginning to feel that traveling by canoe had some advantages? No, it couldn't be. She stood and put a pot of water on to heat so they could wash the dishes.

After everything was clean, Michael picked up a pack and put it in the canoe. Pema stood on the shore, staring across the lake. "That sky doesn't look real good," she said.

The haze that had obscured the opposite shore of the lake seemed thicker. The sky above it was gray. The air was heavy and thick, its stillness broken by occasional gusts of wind. "I'm a little worried that a storm may be blowing up," she said. "We'd better keep an eye on the sky while we're on the lake. Storms can blow up pretty quickly here. Big Wave may yet live up to its name."

They got in the canoe and set off. They had both put on flannel long-sleeved shirts, for despite the hot, still air, the intermittent squalls of wind were cold.

Pema found that she liked being in the bow. This surprised her, because usually she didn't allow anyone else to be in control on the water. And it was rare that anyone else was in the canoe with her; she went on trips alone, unless she was taking a group of kids out.

But it was sort of fun being in the front. Her sense of being suspended on the water was increased, since other than the bow deck of the canoe, there was nothing before her except water. It was nice, too, to just paddle without having to worry about keeping the canoe on course.

This fact brought another realization to mind. She could paddle without worrying about course because Michael was doing such a good job in the stern. He was doing more than just keeping them on a straight line, he was doing it with confidence. Pema could tell from the way the canoe cut through the water, from the sound the waves sluicing around the bow made, that the craft was happy. The canoe knew she was in good hands.

"You're doing a wonderful job back there," she said.

"I know, my canoe told me."

"It talks to you?" Michael grinned and ran a hand through his curls, which were ruffled by the wind.

"Not in words. But we know how each other feels, she and I. And she likes having you in the stern. I don't understand, for it's only rarely that anyone other than me is sitting back there, and usually she doesn't like the others."

"Others?" Michael felt a faint, heated stirring in his gut. Others had been in her canoe with her, they and her alone out here in the woods of Saskatchewan? Had the others been men?

"Yes, sometimes I bring small groups of kids out on trips." Pema kept up her steady strokes, her paddle

LAKE OF DREAMS

moving through the water and then through the air, water drops flying from its blade. "They're what you'd call disadvantaged kids, from poorer parts of the city. Often they've never been into the bush. It's especially special when they're Native kids, and they can live for a few days the way their ancestors did."

"That sounds wonderful. Do you bring them out here?"

"Oh, no, I always take them on trips closer to Saskatoon. I wouldn't want to do so much driving with them. It is wonderful, I suppose, but I don't do it very often. I really prefer canoeing alone. The kids are pretty good, even the ones that are problems in the city, but they are noisy, and no matter how hard they try, they always leave traces of themselves, you know, broken underbrush, bits of garbage. It's important to me to leave no trace of myself when I move through the bush. And I'm selfish. I get so little time to go on canoe trips, I guess I'd rather be able to come up here, to Meniskamee."

"I don't think you're selfish. No one who gives up time to help poor city kids can be called that."

"Well, maybe." Pema noticed that she had to raise her voice a bit to make sure Michael could hear her. The wind was picking up. "I could do more trips with them, help more of them. It is really rewarding, just to see their eyes when they see a loon diving under the water, or catch their first fish. And the pride they take in learning to handle a canoe. I don't think they succeed in many things in the city, but out here they learn to do things they've never done before, and they do them well."

"I think you're a pretty special person, Pema. You're one of the few who can make a difference in this world. You see a way to make things better, and you actually do it. I think that once you go to grad school, if you really

88 LAKE OF DREAMS

want to, you'll make a difference to the environment, too."

"Yes, well . . ." She gazed across the lake. If she really wanted to. She really wanted to go to grad school, didn't she? But wanting to wasn't enough. She was beginning to think that maybe she never would go. But if she accepted that, her dream would die. And without her dream, wouldn't she die, too?

"Anyway," Michael was saying, "this poor city boy is certainly grateful for what you've done for him."

"You're not a poor city boy." Pema was glad to shake off the melancholy that had threatened to overwhelm her. "You're a rich city boy."

"Maybe in terms of money. But I'm poor in other ways. I've never seen a loon dive under water."

"Oh, you poor, deprived child. Don't worry, I'm sure we'll see loons sometime during the trip."

"I'm serious, though," said Michael, "about being grateful. I'm glad we're here in this canoe. You may not have noticed, but I wasn't real excited about the idea before we left."

"I noticed."

"I will admit, I was upset because I couldn't bring my portable CD player." He laughed. "And I thought riding in a canoe would be cold, wet and cramped. But other than a couple of blisters, I feel really good."

"Do you mean that?" Pema stopped paddling and twisted to look at him.

"Yes." He paused to think. "It's hard to explain. It's as if there's something inside me, something I don't fully understand. You see, it was *my* idea to find a retreat in a natural setting for the seminars. I think that this urge of mine to get part of my job out of the city must relate to something, some need I have, to be closer to a natu-

LAKE OF DREAMS

ral environment. And the longer I'm out here, traveling with you and your canoe, the closer I come to understanding this."

"I see. Oh, Michael, I'm so happy." Pema's smile was brighter than the sun, which was, at the moment, obscured by clouds. "It's something I've always believed. People have—"

Just then a wave slapped the bow of the canoe, sending cold water into her lap.

"Ooh," she gasped. She turned forward again, and saw with dismay that whitecaps were all over the lake. "The wind has really picked up. How could I have been so unobservant? You always have to be on the watch out here. If you're not, well, that's how accidents happen."

The lake was the color of slate, reflecting the dark clouds that had poured across the sky. The wind was blowing steadily, a stream of air that was cold and damp. The surface of the water was no longer a sparkling, dancing sheet. It moved sullenly, up and down, forming itself into waves that rose before the wind until they grew too high even for the power of the coming storm, and they crashed over on themselves in a curling froth of white.

Pema knew she couldn't stop to get rain gear out of the packs, for the wind was too strong. "Get down on your knees." She had to shout to be heard. "The storm won't reach us just yet. Our campsite isn't too far from here. I think if we really paddle we can make it. If you see any lightning, though, take us right in to shore."

They began to paddle, working in rhythm, their bodies moving as one. Shoulders and backs leaned forward, arms plunged paddles into the water, backs and arms pulled back, sending the canoe forward. The canoe began to bob, surging forward up over a wave, racing down the other side.

"Michael," Pema shouted, "try to keep us heading into the waves on an angle. But also, as much as possible, head straight for that group of trees I showed you. That's where the campsite is."

"Aye, aye, ma'am."

She looked at him. There was a gleam in his eyes, and his mouth was open in an exultant grin. His face was dripping with water from spray blown across the canoe by the wind, but he seemed happier and more alive than she had yet seen him. And Pema knew her own face held the same expression.

The wind increased in force, the waves becoming wilder. The canoe was bucking, rolling sideways as well as up and down. "We need to brace," she called. "We're almost there, we can make it! Brace with your paddle when you're at the crest of a wave. Paddle in the trough." She could feel her hair clinging to her back, tendrils whipping in the wind. She was very wet; in the bow, she was directly in the path of spray from every wave the bow hit. But she knew she and Michael together could get through.

They paddled hard. As the canoe climbed a wave, Pema laid her paddle across the gunwales and leaned on it, distributing weight to both sides so the canoe wouldn't roll. Michael was paddling still. As the canoe surged forward, the bow riding down, she took up her paddle and drove the canoe forward while he braced.

The sky grew ever darker. A rumble of thunder was heard, but Pema's anxious eyes saw no sign of lightning. The clouds were thick and heavy, hanging close above the tiny canoe moving through the wind-tossed

LAKE OF DREAMS

lake. The water held by the clouds was ready to be loosed, but still it waited.

Michael could feel the hair on his arms, wet as it was, trying to stand on end. His whole body tingled, for the charged tension in the air caused by the soon to be released furies of the storm was almost tangible. He plunged his paddle into the water, his blood surging through his veins, his muscles singing. He looked at Pema ahead of him, her slender form beneath the wet, clinging shirt moving, paddling, bracing, without a stop. What a woman she was, to have such strength and endurance. What a craft this canoe was, to appear so frail and to withstand the powers unleashed on this lake.

And what a wonderful feeling, to be here, fighting for what was probably his very life, for he knew no one could swim for long in this sort of water, to be pitting himself against nature. For maybe the first time in his life, he, Michael Christie, was fighting something with only his own body, his physical skills and his wits. No games were being played, no rules interfered, no briefcases filled with pieces of paper held any power. It was him, Michael, against the storm. Him, and Pema.

The clump of trees they were heading for grew closer. Still the rain held off. When they reached the shore, Pema and Michael quickly unloaded the gear and carried the canoe well up on the shore, leaving it upside down beneath some low trees.

"Hurry," she called. "Let's set up at least one tent. Those clouds are going to open any second now."

Michael opened a pack and pulled out the blue tent. Working as quickly as they could with their wet, cold hands, he and Pema set up the tent. And just in time, too.

There was a momentary gasp, as though the whole outdoors had sucked in its breath. Then the clouds opened, throwing free their load of water. The wind swooped down, prying at the tent, air fingers reaching to pull it loose from the earth.

Pema grabbed the packs and thrust them into the tent. She scurried into the woods, grabbed some dry wood and carried it inside, too. Then she looked for Michael.

He was standing on the shore of the lake, close to the waves that threw themselves at him, surging at the land only to fall and die, running, hissing and bubbling back to the madness that was the lake. He had taken off his shirt and stood, clad only in his jeans, his body exposed to the elements.

She went down toward him, worried. What would he think about canoeing now? Despite her initial desire to prove to him how uncomfortable and inconvenient traveling to Meniskamee could be, she had felt a joy when he told her how canoeing was meeting some need deep inside him. It was a bond between them. But it was easy to enjoy a canoe trip when the sun was warm and the lake was a calm sheet of dancing sparkles. This was part of canoeing, too. You took what the environment threw at you, good and bad.

Michael's jeans were soaked through, clinging tightly to the lines of his hips and legs. Water dripped from his hair, off his nose, down his back. He raised his hands over his head, and Pema saw the muscles cord in his arms as he shook his fists at the heavens. Then he turned to her, and she saw that he was laughing.

Chapter Five

The atmosphere in the tent was distinctly humid. It was also crowded. Two packs, two sleeping bags, life jackets, a pile of dry wood and two very wet people took up a lot of room.

Pema scrambled around on her knees, moving things, trying to make space for each of them to sit down. She dug in a pack and pulled out a tin plate and a candle. She took a match out of its waterproof container and lit it, burning the bottom of the candle until the wax was sticky enough to hold it to the plate. Then she lit the candle.

The small flame flickered then burned steadily. Shadows danced against the walls of the tent. The rain drummed fiercely against the outer nylon fly, but inside the small tent all was dry and cozy.

"We should get out of our wet things," said Pema. She pulled a towel out of the pack and began rubbing her

94 LAKE OF DREAMS

hair. She had taken it out of its clip, and it hung, dark with water, clinging to her shoulders and back.

"Good idea," said Michael. "I hadn't realized how cold and heavy a wet pair of jeans could be." His hands went to his belt buckle.

Pema swallowed in a mouth suddenly dry and looked quickly at her lap. Of course, they had to get out of their wet things, and, also of course, neither of them could go outside to do it. The idea of the operation was to get dry, after all, and going outside would definitely not accomplish that. Besides, no girl growing up with four brothers was a stranger to the male body, so why was she suddenly blushing and looking away like a girl fresh out of a convent?

She heard him slip the jeans off and rummage in his pack for dry clothes. "What should I do with these wet things?" he asked.

"Oh, I..." She lifted her eyes just a little. Michael sat across from her, his legs bent in front of him, as he pulled on a dry pair of pants. In the flickering light of the candle, his skin was yellow and brown. The planes of muscle in his shoulders and chest stood out in sharp relief against the shadows. He began to get to his knees to pull the pants all the way up. She did not look away.

His hips were lean and flat, his buttocks rounded with muscles, hollow on the side as he tensed a leg to slide the pants up over it. He did up the button and fly and sat again, turning to grin at her. "Well?" he said, holding up the sodden mass of his jeans.

"Oh, uh, I guess you may as well toss them outside. They won't dry much in here. When the rain stops, we'll make a fire and dry our things then."

LAKE OF DREAMS

Michael unzipped the tent enough to toss his jeans outside. "Here, give me your things, too, while I've got the door open."

He was still leaning toward the front of the tent, his back to her. Pema wriggled out of her jeans and flannel shirt. She wrapped her towel around her body and thrust the wet clothes at Michael. He put them outside and turned to her.

"What about your underthings?" he asked. "You can't keep them on, they'll be wet and cold. Look at you, you're shivering already."

Pema clutched her towel under her chin and reached underneath to unclasp her bra.

Michael watched, a grin spreading across his face. "Surely you're not shy. A woman of nature like you, don't you know the human body is merely another life form?"

She glared at him. She had the bra undone and had slipped it off, but if she tried to get on her knees to remove her panties, the towel, held to her only by the grip of her chin, would hang forward in a narrow stream of cloth, covering next to nothing.

"Pema," he said, "don't be shy. Your body is beautiful, and I meant what I said. It's natural, everyone has a body. But if you want, I'll turn around."

Pema thought. She realized she probably looked ridiculous, her head clamped to her chest, trying to hide behind a little scrap of terry towel. And Michael was right, her body was nothing to be ashamed of. It was part of her, part of the natural environment. She lifted her chin.

Michael drew in his breath. He forced his face to remain expressionless, his breathing to stay steady. After his little speech about bodies being simply natural, nothing to be remarked upon, he could hardly start to pant over hers. But he wished he could.

She was magnificent. This morning he had caught a glimpse of her during her swim, but now she was revealed in her entirety. Her skin had the sheen of satin; her limbs were long and lithe. Her breasts stood out, high and firm, and her waist was narrow beneath the jut of her ribs. Michael felt his stomach muscles clench. He wished his pants weren't so tight. He fumbled in his pack for a shirt, which he put on, leaving it hanging loose over his jeans.

Pema pulled a large T-shirt over her head and knelt so it could fall around her. It hung to her thighs. Then she unrolled her sleeping bag.

"I'll stay in here to keep warm until the storm ends." She thrust her legs into the bag and pulled it up to her waist. "There. Boy, what I wouldn't give for a hot cup of tea."

"That would be nice. But it probably wouldn't be a good idea to make a fire in here, even though you so thoughtfully brought some wood in." Michael couldn't take his eyes off her. Little tendrils of hair were beginning to dry and were fluffing around her face. In the candlelight, her hair was full of gold highlights, and her eyes looked smoky and mysterious.

"No, definitely not a good idea." Pema wasn't really sure if what she said made sense. Her mind was not paying attention, her ears weren't listening, her eyes were drawn to his. Green, so green they were, like emeralds, glowing in the dark. She wanted to put out a finger, to brush the half-circle of his lashes, so thick and dark. She wanted to trail that finger down his nose, over his cheekbone, to feel the dark bristles that were coating his cheeks and jaw. She wanted to place the tip of that fin-

The more you love romance . . . the more you'll love this offer

FREE!

Mail this heart today! (See inside)

Join us on a Silhouette® Honeymoon
and we'll give you
4 Free Books
A Free Victorian Picture Frame
And a Free Mystery Gift

IT'S A SILHOUETTE HONEYMOON— A SWEETHEART OF A FREE OFFER!
HERE'S WHAT YOU GET:

1. Four New Silhouette Romance™ Novels—FREE!

Take a Silhouette Honeymoon with your four exciting romances—yours FREE from the Silhouette Reader Service™. Each of these hot-off-the-press novels brings you the passion and tenderness of today's greatest love stories...your free passports to bright new worlds of love and foreign adventure.

2. Lovely Victorian Picture Frame—FREE!

This lovely Victorian pewter-finish miniature is perfect for displaying a treasured photograph. And it's yours FREE as added thanks for giving our Reader Service a try!

3. An Exciting Mystery Bonus—FREE!

You'll be thrilled with this surprise gift. It is useful as well as practical.

4. Free Home Delivery!

Join the Silhouette Reader Service™ and enjoy the convenience of previewing 6 new books every month delivered right to your home. Each book is yours for only $2.25* each, a saving of 34¢ each off the cover price per book—and there is no extra charge for postage and handling. It's a sweetheart of a deal for you! If you're not completely satisfied, you may cancel at any time, for any reason, simply by sending us a note or shipping statement marked "cancel" or by returning any shipment to us at our cost.

5. Free Newsletter!

You'll get our monthly newsletter, packed with news about your favorite writers, upcoming books, even recipes from your favorite authors.

6. More Surprise Gifts!

Because our home subscribers are our most valued readers, when you join the Silhouette Reader Service™, we'll be sending you additional free gifts from time to time—as a token of our appreciation.

START YOUR SILHOUETTE HONEYMOON TODAY— JUST COMPLETE, DETACH AND MAIL YOUR FREE-OFFER CARD

*Terms and prices subject to change without notice. Sales tax applicable in NY. Offer limited to one per household and not valid to current Silhouette Romance™ subscribers. All orders subject to approval.

© 1991 HARLEQUIN ENTERPRISES LIMITED

Get your fabulous gifts ABSOLUTELY FREE!
MAIL THIS CARD TODAY.

DETACH AND MAIL TODAY!

GIVE YOUR HEART TO SILHOUETTE

Yes! Please send me my four Silhouette Romance™ novels FREE, along with my Free Victorian Picture Frame and Free Mystery Gift. I wish to receive all the benefits of the Silhouette Reader Service™ as explained on the opposite page.

PLACE HEART STICKER HERE

NAME _____
(PLEASE PRINT)

ADDRESS _____ APT. _____

CITY _____ STATE _____

ZIP CODE _____

215 CIS ADMT
(U-SIL-R-01/92)

SILHOUETTE READER SERVICE "NO-RISK" GUARANTEE

— There's no obligation to buy—and the free gifts remain yours to keep.
— You pay the low subscribers-only price and receive books before they appear in stores.
— You may end your subscription any time by sending us a note or shipping statement marked "cancel" or by returning any shipment to us at our cost.

© 1991 HARLEQUIN ENTERPRISES LIMITED

PRINTED IN U.S.A.

START YOUR
SILHOUETTE HONEYMOON TODAY.
JUST COMPLETE, DETACH AND MAIL YOUR
FREE-OFFER CARD.

If offer card below is missing write to:
Silhouette Reader Service, 3010 Walden Ave.,
P.O. Box 1867, Buffalo, NY 14269-1867.

DETACH AND MAIL TODAY!

BUSINESS REPLY MAIL
FIRST CLASS MAIL   PERMIT NO. 717   BUFFALO, NY

POSTAGE WILL BE PAID BY ADDRESSEE

SILHOUETTE READER SERVICE
3010 WALDEN AVE
PO BOX 1867
BUFFALO NY 14240-9952

NO POSTAGE
NECESSARY
IF MAILED
IN THE
UNITED STATES

LAKE OF DREAMS 97

ger on his mouth, feel the soft firmness of his lips, feel the wetness when he parted his lips and took her finger in.

She heard Michael take in a sudden deep breath. Her gaze left his mouth, leaping to his eyes. And the hunger she saw there filled her body with heat.

She knew suddenly that everything hinged on her. If she reached out to him in any way, even just with that finger, he would come to her. He would climb over the packs lying between them, he would push the pile of dry wood over, he would lower his body onto the sleeping bag that held hers. Oh, how she wanted him. But she did not move.

She felt a little like a small furry creature, transfixed by the green eyes of a coal black panther. For she, a big girl now at twenty-five, was still a virgin. And until now, she had never regretted it.

Her brothers had insisted that one of them accompany her on dates until she was seventeen. And when she was finally deemed trustworthy to be out on her own, even if she had wanted to betray that trust, she couldn't have. It was well known in the circles in which she moved that she had four very large brothers. No boy that she ever met would dare to try anything. And so now, even though her body ached with a woman's passion, she was paralyzed with a girl's fear. And the moment passed.

Michael stirred, reaching for a pack, pulling out a bag of dried fruit. "Hungry?" he asked. "There's this, and I noticed some pita bread and peanut butter. I can't give you tea, but if you wait, I'll get some guaranteed pure fresh water." Taking a cup, he held it out through the mouth of the tent.

She giggled. "I'd love some pure water. It doesn't come much fresher than that."

98   LAKE OF DREAMS

"Straight from the clouds to you."

Pema's mouth lost its smile. What nonsense they were talking. But she didn't know how else to deal with the tension between them that hung still in the small tent. She took a handful of dried fruit and leaned back against one of the packs. Closing her eyes, she chewed her way through a piece of apricot and listened to the sounds of the rain on the tent, the wind whipping the leaves of the trees overhead.

"I used to love being in a tent during a storm when I was little. With Grandfather."

"Tell me about him."

Michael's voice was soft, but Pema's eyes opened in surprise. She hadn't realized that she had spoken aloud.

"Grandfather was half Indian. He used to tell me the ancient stories about the spirits, about the spirit of the storm and the spirit of the wind, and how they loved each other, but how each was full of pride and sometimes they had to fight, to show each other how strong and powerful they were. About how they would run together, through the trees, whipping the leaves, over the lakes, lashing the water, and they would scream at one another, each trying to be the loudest. But then they would laugh, for they knew that one without the other was nothing. Storm and wind, both are strong, but it's only when they're together that they reach their full power. And then, linked together, they would leave their playground, the earth, and run back up into the sky, where they lived together, until the next time they felt a need to try to outdo one another."

As if in corroboration of her tale, there came a rumble of thunder. At the same time, a furious gust of wind tore at the tent, trying to pull it loose and set it free. But then the thunder died away, the wind lessened, and the

LAKE OF DREAMS 99

patter of the rain was softer. The storm was coming to an end.

"Grandfather took me to Meniskamee whenever he could. I helped him build the cabin. The two of us, we did it together. I was very small, and maybe I wasn't much help, but he made me feel I was.

"He had a strong sense of himself as part of the environment, a life spirit no more or less important than any other life spirit. He taught me how to be one with the world he lived in, how to move through the bush, how to find food, how to find shelter. He taught me how to see, hear, how to use my nose. He taught me how to be."

Pema's voice wafted through the small enclosed space of the tent, filling Michael's mind with visions. He could see the small girl, her hair so bright, and the older, darker-skinned man. They walked through the trees, the man stopping to point out a small plant that could be used to make a medicinal balm. Then he stood up, straight and tall, his hand outstretched, leading her wondering eyes to the sight of a vee of Canada geese flying overhead.

"He made me what I am," Pema said. "Or rather, he allowed me to be what I am. When I was with Grandfather I could be myself. There were no preconceptions, no ideas that I couldn't do certain things because I was a girl. He saw me for what I am, he took what I had to give and never looked for anything else. Three years ago, we built my canoe. He was getting very old, but I never really thought about it. His hands, even though they were callused and gnarled, were so strong when we cut the narrow strips of wood, so gentle when we carved the thwarts and seats. But he knew he was getting old. And then, last year..." Pema felt her voice thicken with tears.

Michael said nothing. He knew that even though it was painful, she wanted to tell him.

"He told me it was time for him to rejoin his ancestors. He wanted me to bring him out here, so he could die in the place he loved best, surrounded by the spirits who knew him best. And we came, our last time to paddle these waters together. And when we got to Meniskamee, we took a last walk together. I was hoping it wasn't true, that he wasn't going to leave me. He seemed so strong, walking straight like he always did. But when we got back to the cabin, he told me to leave. He needed to be alone. I left, I couldn't deny him his wish. But when I got to Laughing Spirit, to the rapids, I couldn't stay away. Maybe he was ill, or in pain. Maybe he needed me. I went back."

Pema stared into the small light of the candle. It burned brightly, a tall, steady flame. "He wasn't there. I looked all over for any trace of him. I was afraid of what I might find, but I looked anyway. And I found nothing. He was truly gone."

She felt warm arms wrap around her. A strong, hard chest was there in front of her, and she buried her face in it. "He didn't leave me alone, though," she said. "I can feel him with me, especially when I'm there. He is one now, with all the spirits he loved so well." And then she lifted her head and blindly searched out Michael's mouth with hers.

She kissed him, her mouth hot and moist against his. Her hands reached up, cradling his head, pulling him even closer. She kissed his chin, his cheeks, his nose. She was on fire, the flame of the candle burning deep within her, only a thousand times brighter. She was filled with a need so strong it hurt.

LAKE OF DREAMS 101

Michael felt her need. He pulled her into his arms, her legs sliding out of the sleeping bag until she sat across his lap. The feel of her buttocks pressing into his thighs, the scent of her hair, the warm moisture of her skin, were filling his being. He captured her mouth with his, drinking deeply, while his hands slipped under her T-shirt, caressing the smoothness of her back.

Pema felt as if a wildness within her had been unleashed. She reached for his shirt, undoing buttons, pulling the cloth aside. She pressed her face against the wiry hairs that covered the firm muscles, opening her mouth to taste him. She circled one of his nipples with her tongue, and heard his sharp intake of breath.

Michael was losing control, he knew it. The whole world contained nothing but him and her, the flicker of the candle and the patter of the rain. He wanted this woman. And it would be so easy, the two of them, alone here with the wind and the storm. But he was coming to know Pema, to know her well. He sensed and understood her need. And he knew it would be wrong for him to take her.

He wanted to take her lake from her. No matter how much he cared for her, the lake was the purpose of the trip, and he would not be swayed. But if he made love to Pema, if she gave herself to him, it would be as if he had somehow taken everything from her, lake and body, too. He could not be so cruel. For he knew that they could have no future. She could have no place in his life in Toronto, and he had no permanent life here. She was locked into her world, her life of small town and farm, teaching and canoeing. Her chains were so strong that they kept her even from living her dream. How could she possibly set herself free enough to enter a larger world, with him?

102   LAKE OF DREAMS

Pema tilted her head back. "Grandfather always told me that when you love enough, you know what is right." She smiled.

But Michael did not believe it. Love is not enough, he thought. You have to be logical and practical, too.

And so he pulled her against him, her head resting on his shoulder, and he stroked her hair and whispered sweet words in her ear until the fires that raged within her quietened. And she fell asleep, cradled against him, before she had a chance to think on what Michael had denied her.

Pema woke early, to the dancing dapples of sun and shadow on the tent walls. Her sleeping bag had been unzipped and carefully laid over her. On the other side of the tent, she could see Michael, in his bag, still asleep.

She watched the shadows sweeping back and forth over the tent. She liked waking up to the early sun, listening to the birdcalls, hearing the steady whisper of the lake. So why did she feel a wrongness? Her muscles were tense, and her face felt sore and reddened. But beyond these physical sensations, there was a strong feeling deep in her core that she had wanted something, something she'd waited for for a long time, and it hadn't come. And then the events of the previous evening came to her in a rush, and she felt her cheeks flame.

There had been the storm, the whipping waves, the lashing wind. There had been the exhilaration and exultation, shared with Michael, of fighting the storm and winning. There had been the furies, equal in power to those outside the tent, unleashed within her when she had reached for Michael and kissed him. Oh, how she had wanted him. And what a beautiful feeling it had

LAKE OF DREAMS 103

been, to feel the want, the need, running golden through her veins. But he hadn't wanted her.

He had been very nice, holding her, cradling her, soothing her. But he had treated her like a child, like the little girl her brothers knew her as. Michael had not treated her like the woman she knew she was.

And so when Michael stirred and turned to her with a sleepy smile, she glared at him. "I'm going out for a swim," she said. "And if you know what's good for you, you'll stay in here until I get back. I want no Peeping Toms today."

She ran down the bank to the water, the grass damp on her bare feet. Shedding the T-shirt, she plunged into the lake, feeling the water cool her heated body. The lake this morning showed no sign of the wild gray tossing mass of water it had been last night. The water was calm, a soft mist rising from its surface. The sun glinted gold on the ripples formed by Pema's passing through the water.

She swam a long way along the shore, feeling her muscles working, her arms pulling, her legs kicking. It felt good to be stretching and flexing, her mind losing its thoughts to the needs of the physical demands of moving through water. But when she came out at last, the water running in streams over her breasts, dripping from her hair, the pain of rejection was still strong.

Her bad mood didn't improve as the day wore on. The tent had been damaged during the storm—a peg tab had been pulled out, tearing off a piece of tent fabric with it. Pema glued on a piece of nylon patching, then sewed the tab on again.

The fire, even with the dry wood she had kept in the tent, was difficult to start. She built racks to hang the wet clothes on. Her jeans, dripping still, were just beginning to dry when the stick holding them up broke, and they fell in the dirt. Pema picked them up and brushed them off and built another rack.

She pulled all the gear out of the tent and saw that the wood had left bits of bark and dirt all over the floor. She cleaned it out and rolled the tent, leaving the fly stretched out to dry. Michael, meanwhile, had boiled some water and made coffee. He handed her a cup and she sat down by the fire, staring at the flames. "That wood you put on is much too big," she said. She gestured at a log with her hand, and hot coffee slopped onto her skin. She sucked on the burn and glared at Michael as if it had been his fault. "You never need to use sticks that are bigger than this one. It's just a waste of wood. Even though it's dead wood, it still shouldn't be wasted."

Michael looked at the wet clothes drying by the fire. Steam was rising from the cloth. He looked back at Pema, a little smile quirking his mouth.

"What are you looking at?" she demanded.

"I'm surprised there's not steam rising from you, also," he said.

"Very funny." She drank her coffee, feeling its warmth travel down into her stomach.

Pema wanted to make it to the end of the Laughing Spirit River that day. It wasn't even a full day's paddle to the campsite there, but she found she couldn't sit still any longer. They ate breakfast, they washed the dishes, they loaded the canoe, and then there was nothing to do but watch the clothes dry. The minute they were done, Pema jumped to her feet and doused the fire, and they were off.

After a short paddle they came to the portage that would take them to Laughing Spirit. Pema began to pull on the side of the canoe, readying it for the lift that would get it on to her thighs, when she saw large hands appear on the gunwale next to hers.

"I will carry the canoe," Michael said.

"No, you won't."

He left his hands where they were. He waited, his body still, but Pema could feel the coiled tension in the length of his hip and thigh pressed against hers.

"Don't you dare," she said.

But he took the canoe from her, pushing her aside with his large body. As she watched, her eyes bright with fear and anger, he lifted the canoe onto his bent legs and then effortlessly rolled it onto his shoulders.

"What about your pack?" she demanded. "Am I expected to carry two?"

Swearing under his breath, Michael lowered the canoe to the ground, shouldered his pack, and returned the canoe onto his back. "I would have thought a woman with your many talents could carry two packs easily. After all, you're not a soft city yuppie like I am. But maybe you have other softnesses I don't know about. If you do, you sure hide them well. You can carry the paddles and life jackets, I assume?" And he was off down the trail before she had the chance to think of a stinging comeback.

This portage was longer, a little over a mile. Pema walked along, stumbling over the occasional root. Michael kept moving at a steady pace, his long strides covering the ground smoothly. She wished that he would trip and fall flat on his face, except that if he did, the canoe might be damaged. She followed behind him, quietly fuming.

When the canoe was floating on the waters of the Laughing Spirit River, loaded and ready to go, Pema got into the stern. She glared at Michael, her eyes daring him to object, but he ignored her, picked up his paddle and climbed into the bow. As they got under way, Pema realized she might have made a mistake, for now she had to look at him all day. His broad back looked so warm and strong, his black hair curling down over his neck. He wore a light blue T-shirt, and its thin material clung to his skin, molding itself over the planes of muscle. Despite herself, Pema had to admit that for a soft city body, his was pretty hard. His arms swung forward and back, handling the paddle with an ease that made Pema grind her teeth, even though she knew that in part her teaching could take credit for his skill. But he was a city man; he had no right be so at home in a canoe. Especially not in her canoe.

She tried not to look at him, to distract herself by watching the shores of the river go by. Laughing Spirit was a beautiful river, narrow and swift. The forest came right to the river's edge, the trees bending their branches over the blue water, watching their reflections and whispering to the ripples. Birds called in among the leaves, and Pema had occasionally seen deer come to the water's edge to drink. The water was fairly shallow, and if she looked down, she could see fish swimming, their shapes dark against the tan and gold of the sandy bottom.

But none of the sights and sounds that normally so delighted her heart had any effect today. She dug her paddle into the water, listening to the *cloop* it made, and watched the little whirlpools of water left by the passage of the blade as they swirled away behind the canoe. She paddled hard, making bigger whirlpools, feeling the strain spread over her shoulders and down her arms. She looked at the trees and listened to the birds,

LAKE OF DREAMS 107

but the wonders of the world she was passing through did not speak to her, did not enter her being. They were merely there, and she looked and listened only to avoid looking at Michael.

They stopped in a grassy clearing for lunch. The meal was silent and quick, both of them sitting on the soft green, eating and avoiding one another's eyes. They washed up and Pema went off into the forest a little way to relieve herself while Michael put the cooking things in the pack.

The forest was cool and green, and the ground beneath her feet was soft. None of this registered in her mind, though, and when she squatted behind a clump of trees, a cloud of mosquitoes appeared out of nowhere, whining and settling with joy on her skin. She finished quickly and stood, pulling up her pants with one hand, the other flapping and slapping at mosquitoes. She realized that she had been bitten a number of times in a very sensitive area, and one in which it was usually embarrassing to scratch. Her mood was not improved when she returned to the canoe.

She picked up the pack to put it in the canoe, and a sharp edge from the cooking pot dug into her side. She turned on Michael in a fury, knowing much of the anger she felt was directed at herself. She was acting abominably, but the pain of Michael's rejection of her last night, added to her conflict over losing her lake, was just too much. She spoke, realizing she would regret her angry words, but unable to stop herself. "Can't you do anything right? Don't you even know how to put a few small things into a pack?"

For Michael, this was enough. He had spent the whole day so far putting up with her bad mood, paddling while feeling green fire from her eyes boring into his back. He didn't know what her problem was, but any sympathy he might have had was long gone.

"You are acting like a spoiled brat," he said, his voice cold. "No wonder your brothers treat you like a little child, because that's exactly how you act."

Pema's feelings of regret vanished. "You leave my brothers out of this. At least they knew how to love a child. Not like your big-city family, so concerned with making more money than they need that they had no time to look after their only child."

"My parents, busy as they were, were still able to instill in me a sense of worth, and the power to go for what I wanted. Your brothers have raised you to be nothing more than a decorative ornament."

Pema was almost jumping up and down, she was so angry. All the frustrations of the day, and of the evening before, were now coming out, aimed at Michael. "Why did your parents even have you, if they had no time for you?"

"And why, if your upbringing was so wonderful, do you not have the self-confidence to go after your dream?"

Her face whitened, her eyes very round and green against her pale skin. Michael knew he had gone too far. But she said nothing. She whirled away from him, splashing through the water to the canoe. He picked up the pack and followed her.

They set off down the river, the water laughing and slapping against the bow of the canoe. The air was warm and sweet, the soft breeze bearing the scents of the forest. But neither of them noticed.

Michael picked up a handful of water and splashed it on his face. The cool felt good, but it did not help to cool his anger. Pema didn't help, either, when, from behind

LAKE OF DREAMS 109

him, she said, "Who are you to talk to me about dreams anyway? You wouldn't know a genuine dream if it jumped out of this river and slapped you in the face."

"I don't think you know about dreams, either." Michael did not twist to face her, but he knew his words were forceful enough for her to hear. "Your plan to go to graduate school may have been a dream once, but now it's nothing more than a worn-out teddy bear. A toy for a child."

"How dare you—" she began, but he swept on.

"A dream is only a dream if you work to make it come true. If it's only something you keep to comfort yourself, then it's nothing more than a security blanket."

"You know nothing!" Pema struggled to keep her voice under control. "My dream, even though I haven't yet made it come true, is a real dream, a dream to make the world better, not only for me but for all living things."

"How noble." Michael's voice was tight. "It's all very well for you to talk of how unselfish and wonderful you are, but it isn't going to happen, is it? It hasn't happened yet. You keep putting it off. You obviously like to talk and think about how special you are a lot more than you like to actually do something."

Pema was so mad that she considered rolling the canoe and tipping Michael out.

"And," he continued, "I know why you're all talk and no action. It's because you're afraid. Yes, Pema Robinson, the intrepid outdoorswoman, is scared. You're—"

At that point a large amount of water, scooped up and flung from Pema's paddle, landed on his back. Michael forced himself not to flinch. He would not give her the

110   LAKE OF DREAMS

satisfaction of seeing that her childish act of temper had any effect on him. They paddled on in silence.

Since they were both so angry, their paddle strokes were longer and harder than they would have been, and the canoe moved along at a fast pace. Pema realized that they would reach their campsite earlier than she had expected.

The sun, flashing off the blade of Michael's paddle, glared into her eyes. She was getting a little tired, but she refused to let up, to slow down her pace. If he could keep paddling so hard and so fast, well, so could she. But she did feel a sense of relief when, from up ahead of them, she heard the first sounds of the Laughing Spirit Rapids.

The sound, like a whisper in the distance, grew to a gurgle and a roar. Pema brought the canoe in at a clearing on the shore just above the rapids.

Michael climbed onto a rock that jutted out at the beginning of the fast water. He had never seen anything like this stretch of river. The water seethed and boiled, ramming itself against rocks and shooting into the air. It foamed and bubbled, coursing over rocks or squeezing between boulders in a black stream, looking deceptively calm and smooth. The air was full of moisture, water and spray jumping up from the rocks only to be caught and tossed by the wind. His face was damp, and his ears were full of the sound of the rushing, twisting water. And his heart was full of desire. A desire to tackle the Laughing Spirit, to enter this watery madness and master it.

"Are you coming?" Pema's voice broke into his thoughts. She had put on her pack and picked up the canoe. "Our campsite is where Laughing Spirit comes out into Clarendon Lake. We have a portage to do."

LAKE OF DREAMS 111

Michael picked up his pack. The excitement and magic of the rapids obviously hadn't entered her soul. He suspected that her bad mood was in part due to what had, or hadn't, happened between them last night. He was a little sorry for some of the things he'd said in anger while they were paddling, but not too sorry. Perhaps those things needed to be said. In any case, his anger was gone now, replaced by the roar and power of the rapids.

After they set up camp, he wandered to where the fast water emptied into the lake. From here he could see a good way up the rapids, up to where it came around a bend. He could see why it was called white water. The water, as it spilled and churned among the rocks, was frothed into white foam and bubbles. As his eye roamed over the rushing water, he began to pick out areas that didn't seem quite as wild, places where the water ran a little smoother, or where there didn't seem to be quite as many rocks sticking up. And most of those places looked wide enough for a canoe to pass through.

He turned to Pema, who was sitting by the shore of the lake, throwing pebbles into the water. "How come we didn't canoe through those rapids?" he asked.

"We didn't because I don't do it with an inexperienced paddler in the canoe. I usually do run them, when I come here on my own."

"I would like to try."

Pema looked up at Michael. He stood, balanced easily on the wet rock, his feet far apart, planted firmly on the slippery surface. His hair, curlier than ever, tossed by the wind, was dampened by the spray floating down the rapids, and small curls were plastered to his forehead. His jaw, darkened by beard stubble, looked leaner and harder, the angular planes of his facial bones high-

112   LAKE OF DREAMS

lighted by the dark shadow. He looked tough and capable.

She didn't like him looking like that. He looked good, too good. He was too attractive. She wished to have no kindly thoughts about him at all. So she laughed and said, "You? It takes a lot of practice and skill to learn to handle a canoe in white water like that. It isn't like driving your fancy car in rush hour traffic, you know. Just because you learned to handle a paddle adequately on smooth lakes doesn't mean you now know everything."

"Everyone has to start somewhere," he said. "I'd like to try."

"Well, forget it." Her words were clipped. "You may think you know everything, including how to run my life, but you don't. You know nothing about my dream, and you know nothing about me. And most of all, you know nothing about running rapids."

She stood up and began to walk along the shore of the lake, away from the camp. Tears were burning beneath her eyelids and threatening to fall. She didn't like this foul mood she was in, but she didn't seem to be able to do anything about it.

She moved along the shore. Right now she needed to be alone.

Michael watched her retreating back. So she thought he knew nothing, did she? Did she think he should be afraid? Content to cower meekly until she deigned to let the soft city man try a new experience?

He turned to the rapids. The rushing and roaring seemed to enter his soul, filling his mind with turbulence and excitement. He stepped into the water, his bare feet gripping the rocks on the bottom. He felt his body thrill to the feel of the water rushing past his legs. It pulled at him, hard and cool, trying to dislodge him, to

LAKE OF DREAMS

make him fall. But it couldn't. He took a few steps, feeling the strength in his muscles as his legs withstood the force of the water. Then he returned to the camp. He picked up a life jacket and a paddle, then lifted the canoe. He glanced quickly around, but Pema had disappeared along the lakeshore. He stepped onto the portage trail, his feet taking him back to where the Laughing Spirit Rapids began.

Chapter Six

Michael eased the canoe into the water just above the rapids. He decided to paddle a little way upstream first. He remembered how it had been when he'd paddled the canoe alone, when Pema had tried to swim across the lake. He had to admit, he admired her spirit, even though she'd been so unpleasant today. How could such a determined woman have let fear stand in the way of following her dream? He was sorry she hadn't completed her swim. Succeeding probably would have been good for her self-esteem.

Paddling, he recalled the control a single canoeist had over his craft. The canoe responded to his every whim. He knew he could do it. He was in control.

Before launching the canoe, he had had a good look at the course of the river through the rapids, picking out the best spots for the canoe to pass through. Now, as he approached the first turbulence, he reviewed his mental map.

LAKE OF DREAMS

The first obstacle was a drop, but it wasn't very steep. He could see it approach, a line across the water. Looking ahead down the river, he could see the trees and brush coming down to the shore. Straight ahead, though, across the line on the water, he realized he was looking at the trees from a point on their trunks; the roots and brush were below his line of vision. And then he knew, with a shock of thrill, that he was here, in the rapids, the canoe and him alone with no way out except to move ahead.

As he got closer to the drop, he could see the foam and waves flicking across the line and hear the water gurgling as it fell. He remembered that the water had seemed to fall more smoothly over to the left, and so he worked to move the canoe in that direction.

This wasn't as easy as he had thought. The river narrowed here, and the current was swift and strong. It had the canoe well in its grip. Michael fought the current, using draw strokes, his muscles cording as he pulled to bring the canoe sideways. Beneath his knees, he could feel the slender craft twisting as it tried to follow the will of its true element, the water. It felt like a live being, rolling, rocking, surging through the water. But he was the stronger, and the canoe moved slowly toward the left side of the river as it neared the drop.

Michael felt the bow tip forward and plunge swiftly down. And then the rest of the canoe, with him riding it, was slipping, sliding, pouring over the rocky edge amidst a plume of foam and a wash of spray.

As suddenly as it had begun, he was over the drop. The waves boiled and surged around the canoe, and it seemed to Michael that the water was speaking to the boat, sharing the wondrous thing they had just done together. The river laughed. The canoe sang. And Mi-

116 LAKE OF DREAMS

chael felt that he, too, shared the excitement and the glory. He laughed out loud.

But there was no time to revel in his first success. Already the water had caught up the canoe and was sweeping it forward, toward a part of the river that was scattered with boulders. Michael tried to remember which had seemed to be the best rocks to pass between, but things looked different from down here, on the level of the water, than from when he stood above on shore.

A rock was suddenly dead ahead! He gave a quick flip to his paddle, and the canoe twisted and passed by the rock. But there was another. A turn the other way. This time, though, the current pushed against the canoe and it didn't turn quite enough. Michael heard a harsh scrape as the canoe went by that rock.

But he was doing it. Reaching with the paddle, pulling, backing up, sweeping, he was getting through the rocks. Suddenly he was thrown forward. He grabbed the gunwale to steady himself. The canoe had run into a submerged stone, one he had been unable to see. Luckily, he had held on to the paddle. He knelt again, looking at the river with a new wariness born of respect.

The air was full of the sound of rushing water, of roars and gurgles as it poured over and around the rocks and shot into the air. Michael brushed his dripping hair out of his eyes. At times he seemed to be lower than the surface of the water as the boat plunged into a trough between higher rocks over which the water boiled and bubbled. He was blinded for a moment as a wave leaped up and slapped him in the face. Rubbing the streaming water from his eyes, he saw he was approaching the bend in the river.

The turn was a sharp one, and as it curved the water was channeled into a narrow passage that flowed be-

LAKE OF DREAMS   117

tween two large rocks and dropped into a chute. Michael had seen from the shore that the space between the two rocks was very narrow, but there was room for a canoe, provided he entered the passage straight on. But what he didn't know was that the current didn't approach the drop straight on. Instead, it eddied into the curve of the turn, spinning in a circle around the bend, before it continued down. A more experienced canoeist would have known this. But Michael did not.

He paddled toward the chute, pulling with long, straight strokes to keep his heading. The current pulled at the tail of his canoe so that the craft moved forward, but at an angle. Michael fought hard to keep his heading, plunging his paddle deep into the rushing water, pulling hard, but he was moving too fast, and as the canoe twisted, the side of the hull banged hard against one of the large rocks. The canoe was trapped sideways, the current forcing it against the two rocks.

Michael reached out as far as he could, trying to pull at the water and turn the canoe. But the water rushing under the trapped canoe was forcing the boat into a roll. The upstream gunwale was being lowered toward the rushing water.

The first water splashed in. It poured over the side of the canoe in a rush. The canoe quickly filled and completed its roll. Michael was flung into the rushing torrent.

He was able to take in a lungful of air before he went under. He tightened his muscles, trying to swim, but the current was too strong and he felt his body scrape beneath the still-trapped canoe. As he passed by, he grabbed a thwart. His momentum pulled the canoe free, and it began to move between the rocks and into the chute. Michael lost his grip on the canoe as first it, and then he, shot forward and down.

Michael thought that his lungs would burst. He tried desperately to bring his head up so that he could breathe again to continue his desperate fight. But in the madness that was the water at the bottom of the chute, he couldn't even tell which way was up. The water plunged straight to the bottom of the deep pool that had formed there before turning up and bursting into the air in a storm of spray.

The Laughing Spirit must be really chuckling right now, thought Michael. And then his head hit an underwater rock, and all went black.

Pema was sitting by the shore of Clarendon Lake, on a grassy bank that overlooked an area of stony beach not far from where the Laughing Spirit emptied into the quiet waters of the lake. She was staring idly over the green waters, her fingers plucking at the grass, when she saw a canoe drift by. An empty canoe, half full of water. Her canoe.

She jumped to her feet. What could have happened? How had her canoe gotten into the water all by itself? Michael! She remembered the longing in his eye when he had spoken of shooting the rapids. But surely he couldn't have been that foolish. He wouldn't have dared!

Obviously he had, and now she was the one who had to jump into the lake and swim out to retrieve her canoe. Already she had scrambled down the bank to the pebbly beach and torn her shoes and shorts off. She had to rescue her canoe.

She was hip-deep in the water when she saw a patch of light blue, just the color of the T-shirt Michael had been wearing. And to her horror, she saw that he was still in

LAKE OF DREAMS 119

the shirt. He was floating in the water, his dark hair spread like seaweed around his head. Luckily he was wearing his life jacket and it had done its job, keeping him afloat and rolling him so his face was up. But he wasn't moving at all.

Pema froze. If she didn't go after the canoe, the winds and currents might well carry it far beyond her ability to swim to it. And it was her canoe, her spirit, formed beneath the loving hands of her grandfather. But her hesitation lasted only a moment before she plunged into the water and started swimming with powerful strokes toward Michael's silent form.

She couldn't tell if he was breathing. Blood oozed from a gash on his temple, and his lips were very blue. How long had he been in the water? It was very cold. The hot sun of summer had not yet warmed the waters of this part of the world. Pema grabbed the handle set into the back collar of the life jacket and headed for shore.

She swam, not toward the close stone beach, but in the direction of their camp. She knew she could never hope to carry him once his full weight was on land.

It was a long swim. She didn't know if he even lived, but she fought on desperately. One hand gripped the life jacket, the other pulled against the water. Slowly, too slowly, she moved him steadily toward the camp. Her heart leapt when he feebly struggled for a moment. Pema was very glad that she had set up camp so close to the water's edge. There was only a little distance remaining for her to half drag, half carry Michael up to the tents. Once there she quickly took off his life jacket and stripped him of his wet clothes. The blood was still streaming from the cut on his head, but she knew that there was a more deadly danger to deal with. Hypothermia.

She pulled a sleeping bag out of a tent and unzipped it. Laying it next to Michael, she rolled him onto it and zipped it closed over his body. Then she built a fire. Ignoring all the rules she knew about keeping fires low and using only small pieces of wood, she soon had a roaring blaze going. She pushed the sleeping bag with Michael in it as close as she dared.

He was shivering now, large shudders that had his whole body twitching. She got the other sleeping bag and put it over him. His lips were still blue, his face a terrible chalky white. She reached in the bag and pulled out one of his hands. His fingernails, too, were blue.

She stood and looked down at Michael. He seemed so small, so vulnerable. There was no sign of the power and vitality that normally filled his body. She wanted him to yell at her, his green eyes to snap and flash. But he lay there, so still.

She thought, too, of her canoe, drifting farther out on the lake with every passing second. It might already be too late to retrieve it. And she hadn't been able to see it clearly before, to see if it had been damaged during its passage through the rapids. Perhaps it was beyond repair.

But she couldn't leave Michael. He wasn't regaining warmth quickly enough. His body temperature had dropped far enough that it couldn't rise again without an outside source of heat. Tears began to trickle down her cheeks. Her canoe was gone, maybe lost forever, but that didn't matter. The pain over that loss was nothing compared to her fear of losing the silent, still man lying at her feet. She got the first-aid kit and put it on the

LAKE OF DREAMS

ground. Stripping off her remaining wet clothes, she slipped, naked, into the sleeping bag next to Michael.

She held him in her arms, her breasts crushed against his chest, her legs twined with his. She pressed his cold face to her warm one. Her tears continued to fall, wetting his face with hot moisture. She kissed his cold mouth, those lips that still showed no sign of color. His shivers passed into her body, shaking her, too. Closing her eyes, she held him to her and concentrated on transmitting her body heat to his.

It was the warm wetness of her tears on his face that Michael sensed first. His body did not feel as if it belonged to him. His limbs felt soft and numb and very far away. So he didn't think about them, and concentrated instead on the dampness he felt on his face.

Gradually, other senses began to return, and he could smell the musky scent of someone very near to him. He could hear the steady breathing, a murmur of air that feathered his skin. He could feel the softness of something warm and soft pressed to his body. He struggled to open his eyes.

Pema's first awareness that he had returned to her was the butterfly tickle of his lashes on her cheek. She pulled her head back and found herself gazing into a pair of emerald green eyes.

For a moment neither spoke. Slowly, on each pair of lips, one chiseled and firm, the other soft and pink, a smile grew.

"Oh, Michael," Pema whispered, "I'm so glad. And oh, Michael, I'm so sorry."

"Sorry for what?" Michael found it hard to speak. His mouth was stiff and sore, and his voice seemed to come from a long way off.

122 LAKE OF DREAMS

"If I hadn't been so childish and nasty, if I hadn't put you down about being a city man, if I had agreed to run the rapids with you, and teach you—"

"Hush. If I hadn't been so childish as to think I could do anything, to think I was invincible, if I had only stopped to think about—"

"Hush." Pema put her finger against his lips. And their smiles grew.

"How do you feel?" she asked.

Michael carefully tested his senses and immediately wished he hadn't. But now he had admitted to his body that he was reunited with it, it cried out for attention. "I feel," he said ruefully, "as if I am all one large bruise. And my head! Oh, don't move!" for she had started to sit up. He shifted a bit, until he could rest his cheek on her breast.

"But your head. I should see to it. I haven't even looked to see how bad it is."

"It doesn't matter." He snuggled into his soft pillow. "I can tell it isn't fatal, anyway. What I need most now is some tender loving care."

Pema wrapped her arms around him and held him. She would stay here with him forever if he asked her to.

They lay together quietly for a long time. The sun dipped toward the horizon. At last Pema stirred. "It will be dark soon, and cooler. I should build up the fire. You're warmer now, but we should still be careful. I'll make some hot tea for you. Do you think you can eat anything?"

"Don't go," Michael said. "I still need your warmth, I can tell. I need to feel your silken limbs entwined with mine, I need the softness and sweetness of your body close to mine, I need—"

LAKE OF DREAMS 123

"If you can talk like that, I think you're well enough for me to leave you for a short time. I want to examine your head while it's still light."

Michael made no protest, for when he'd tried to lift himself to complain about her leaving, his head had felt as if it was being bludgeoned with huge hammers. And besides, she had said 'for a short time,' hadn't she?

Pema slipped on a T-shirt and jeans. She built up the fire and put water on to boil. When the water was hot, she dipped a piece of gauze from her first-aid kit in it and began to clean the wound on Michael's temple. It had stopped bleeding but began again as she gently swabbed the skin. She was relieved to see that the cut was not deep, and it didn't look as if the accident had involved anything more than a glancing blow. But the wound was long and jagged, so she cleaned it with disinfectant and closed it as best she could with butterfly closures, covering the whole with a clean gauze pad taped to his temple.

"Do you mind," she asked, "if while it's still warm and light I look at your other cuts and bruises? I just want to make sure that there's nothing serious."

Her ministrations, gentle as they had been, had started Michael's head throbbing, so he merely mouthed the word okay.

She drew off one sleeping bag and unzipped the other. She tried to keep most of his body covered while she examined it, for she wasn't sure if his temperature had yet returned to normal. She ran sure fingers along his limbs, checking for possible broken bones. She cleaned and bandaged a couple of cuts, but other than a large number of areas that would soon be covered with very colorful bruises, she found nothing of concern. Zipping him up again, she noticed the pot of water was boiling and made a cup of tea. She added a large amount of sugar and powdered milk, and set it down by his head.

He was lying with his eyes closed, his skin still very pale. "Michael," Pema whispered, "do you think that if I help you, you can drink some of this tea? It would really be good for you. And I have some aspirin. It's not much, but it would probably help a bit."

He opened his eyes. "My ministering angel," he murmured. He tried to raise himself on his elbows, and she slipped an arm behind his neck and slowly raised his head. Taking the cup of tea in her other hand, she held it to his lips.

"That does feel good." He smiled, trying not to show the pain that pounded in his head and shot down his shoulders along his arms.

She put a couple of aspirin in his mouth and he swallowed them. It did feel good, actually, the warm sweetness of the tea slipping down inside of him, spreading its heat through his stomach.

"Do you want anything to eat?" she asked.

"No, I just want you back in here with me."

"Just a moment and I'll come." She made herself a cup of tea and ate a few mouthfuls of the trail mix. Then she slipped into the sleeping bag with Michael.

"Can you tell me what happened?" Michael asked. "I can't remember very much past when I got the canoe down the first drop."

"I was hoping you could tell me," she said.

"Oh, Pema, your canoe." He raised his head. "What happened to it?"

"Shh. I'm not sure. I'll look tomorrow."

"I wish I could remember." He was feeling better; the sugar in the tea and the aspirin were helping. "I don't like having this blank black hole in my mind."

LAKE OF DREAMS

"You'll remember more as you get better. I think you probably have a concussion. And you were well on your way to hypothermia, too. So you must take it easy and not fret. We're going to stay here a couple of days, and you're going to lie around and relax."

"Pema, Pema. You saved my life, didn't you? I could have died." Michael looked into the darkening sky. He was full of awe that he was here to look at it. "I was incredibly stupid, wasn't I?"

"No, it wasn't you, it was Wendigo."

"Wendigo?"

"He's a spirit. Grandfather told me about him. Him and Naniboujou. Naniboujou the trickster and Wendigo the killer. Every set of treacherous rapids has a Wendigo, waiting. It was he, I'm sure, who did whatever it was that caused you to tip. Maybe he grabbed the canoe or snagged your paddle. And Naniboujou, well, it was he who spilled the hot coffee on my hand this morning and ripped the tent. He's the one who pulls something out of your pack so you leave it behind when you move camp, or who lets the big fish off your hook."

Michael nestled his head into her softness and let her voice flow over and through him. She was speaking now of other spirits, and tricks they had played on her grandfather. He heard only her voice, the words were unnecessary. Her voice spoke of warmth and security, of being there with him, and that was all he needed to hear.

Pema continued to speak, hearing Michael's breathing become slow and steady. The fire glowed red beside her. The sky was dark, and millions of stars shone. Michael was asleep, his cheek pressed on her breast. She fell silent, her hand stroking his hair. The thought of her canoe came to her with a sharp agony. She half sat up, wondering how she could have forgotten it for so long.

126   LAKE OF DREAMS

Michael was out of danger now, surely, so she could go and try to find the canoe. But it was so dark. And then, out of the wind, the voice of her grandfather came to her.

Your place is there, with him, my Pema. Do not worry about your canoe, your place is there.

She lay on her back, feeling peace steal over her. The heaviness of Michael's head was warm on her chest as she stared up at the stars. A shooting star traced a blazing path across the velvety vault.

She replayed in her mind the time she had run her hands and eyes over Michael's naked body, looking for breaks and cuts. But this time, behind her closed eyes, her fingers roamed slowly, lingering, caressing. She felt his smooth skin, taut over the muscles of his arm. She ran her hand over his chest, the wiry dark hair tickling her palm. She felt the ridges of his ribs and then her fingers were tracing the flat planes of his stomach.

This time her movements were not coldly objective, were not performed only with the purpose of seeking out hurts. No, this time her hands and fingers were seeking to draw in, to absorb and enjoy. Her purpose was to caress with a lover's touch.

Pema's eyes opened into the star-filled night. A lover's touch? Love? This was the man who wanted to take her lake from her. He had called her a spoiled child, and worse, treated her like one. He had damaged and lost her canoe. And yet, here she was, pressed against his naked body, wrapped in a sleeping bag. Her head was nestled in the curve where his shoulder joined his neck. She could hear his steady breathing, feel the warm weight of his arm wrapped around her waist. She was happy. Because she loved him. And she fell asleep to dream of the two of them living together at Meniskamee, swimming in the water, exploring the caves in the cliff, walking through the forest and watching the creatures that shared the world with them.

Michael was dreaming, too, but his dream was not nearly so pleasant. He was again in the canoe, he again maneuvered it down the first drop and through the rock garden, and he felt again the exultation of success, of fighting the wild rapids and winning. But the canoe was twisting beneath him, turning and then rolling, only in slow motion this time, so that he saw his body, arms outflung for balance, as he was tipped into the water. And then he was under, and he could hear a cold, gurgly voice, and it was laughing at him.

"So," it whispered, "you thought you could defeat me, did you?" The voice flowed into his ears and exploded there into a million tiny bubbles. "No one can defeat me. No one can fight me and hope to win. It is only when you work with me, when we become one, you and I, that you can hope to succeed." The voice echoed in his ears, growing louder until it was a thunderous roar.

Michael opened his mouth to shout no but the water rushed in, pouring down his throat, and his body was sent tumbling, turning over and over, through the depths of the river.

And then he became aware that he was no longer at the mercy of the rushing water. Something had steadied him; warm arms were holding him. He came to the surface of the water, into the red gold of the sun.

"Shh," Pema said. She held Michael close, her arms wrapped around his chest, her hand reaching behind his back to stroke his hair. "It's okay now, I am here."

"Who are you?" Michael whispered.

128 LAKE OF DREAMS

In his dream, she spoke. "I am Pema. I ride the singing waters in my canoe, and I am one with the wind and the river. I am friend to all who lives."

Michael stirred, still asleep but rising toward the sound of the voice. But the words made no sense. "Who are you?" he said again.

"I am a woman, and I love you." Pema kissed him on his cheek, on each closed eye. Against her breast she could feel that his heart was still beating wildly, so she continued to speak, the words pouring out in a gentle stream, the words that sprang so ready in her heart.

"I love you. I've never said that to any man who is not in my immediate family." She wasn't sure whether she was dreaming. Was she in Michael's dream or was he in hers? Was she really speaking these words, or did she only hear them in her heart? "I've never felt this way before, so free, so joyous, as if all the singing of all the waters between my home and Meniskamee are winging their way out of my heart. Your body is pressed close to mine, skin to skin. Our hearts beat together, the one affected by the other. Our limbs are entangled, my fingers are twined in your hair, our breaths mingle." It didn't matter if she was dreaming. "That is how it should be. It is right."

Michael stopped struggling to waken. He felt that he lay on the surface of a gentle stream, the water all gold and full of laughing bubbles that bore him gently along. His body was wafted by the current, soothed by gentle waves, caressed by warm ripples. Still half asleep, still held by his dream, he didn't listen to the words, but only to the flow of her voice as it ran like clear water between grassy banks and overhanging trees.

Pema awoke to sunshine and cramped muscles. Michael had turned during the night and he lay half on top of her, one heavy leg flung across both her thighs. The events of the previous day and night came to her in a rush. She remembered the words she had spoken in the dark to soothe him from his dream. Her cheeks flamed. She hadn't know she could speak such words, hadn't even known that they could be inside her. Had he heard? Had he understood? They had been the truth, those words, every one of them. She had spoken to him from her heart, with her heart. She loved him.

But what of him, of his heart? She didn't know if he had been conscious during that time in the night. Would he remember her words of love? Would he want to? For she really had no idea what he thought of her. He didn't like her, he had made that clear during the long, unpleasant day they had spent together yesterday. True, after his accident in the rapids he had held her in his arms and had spoken wonderful words, but that could have been merely out of gratitude and relief. She didn't know.

Pema eased herself out of the sleeping bag carefully so as not to disturb Michael. He needed to sleep. She splashed water on her face and pulled on some clothes. She looked at the empty lake and with a sudden clench in her stomach remembered her canoe.

Where was it? Grandfather had come to her during the night and had told her not to worry. But still her feet took her swiftly down to the water's edge.

With one hand over her eyes, shading them from the glare of the reflection of the rising sun, she looked over the lake. It was hard to see, the sun was so very bright, the surface of the lake a sheet of silver and gold. She began to walk along the shore, her eyes never still as they swept back and forth from the shore to the horizon. But she didn't see the long, low hump that would be a canoe floating or half-submerged in the lake.

She came out onto the pebbly beach from which she had first seen the empty canoe swept out of the rapids, from which she had leaped in to the water to rescue Michael. The canoe was there. Pebbles rolled beneath her feet, and she nearly stumbled in her haste to reach it. The wind must have shifted during the night and started blowing onto the shore, or perhaps the waves had nudged it until it was beached. Or else Grandfather had brought it to this spot. Whatever, her canoe was here, upside down, the bow pushed partway onto the beach.

Pema fell to her knees in front of it. Her hands reached out, caressed the smooth hull. It seemed to be all in one piece. It was here.

She pulled the canoe farther up on the beach and walked around it, looking for signs of damage. There were some scratches along one side. Oh, and here, near the bow, a hole. Something hard had run against the canoe, piercing the fiberglass, splintering the wood. The damage was like a bruise on the smooth, golden surface of the hull, the transparent fiberglass white and dented. But it didn't matter. Her canoe was here, it was not lost. It could be made whole again. She lifted it to her shoulders and carried it to camp.

When Michael opened his eyes, the first thing he saw was the canoe. It lay, hull up, on the ground not far from where he was. He saw the hole. He closed his eyes again. His head hurt, his body hurt. But he was here, he was alive, and it was a beautiful day. He could feel the warmth of the sun, and it seemed to him that it was drawing some of the stiffness out of his limbs. He was going to be okay. He would be made whole again. He opened his eyes and focused on the damaged canoe.

LAKE OF DREAMS 131

Pema heard him stir and looked over from where she was crouched, setting out the things she needed to repair the canoe. Michael's eyes were fixed on the hole in the canoe.

"Hello," she said softly. She felt suddenly shy. She and Michael had gone through a lot during the past night; they had traveled together, but she wasn't sure if their paths had ended up in the same place.

"Your canoe," said Michael. "Oh, Pema, I'm so sorry."

"It doesn't matter." She held up a roll of duct tape. "It can be fixed."

He smiled. Her eyes were drawn to him, to the laughter in his eyes. His face was still pale, his growing beard looked very dark, and the white of the bandage on his temple was in sharp contrast to his dark hair. But his eyes glowed green, and his dimple crooked beside his chin, and she felt herself smiling, too.

She made him tea and oatmeal and, sitting on the ground beside him, supported his head while he ate. She changed the bandage on his head, relieved to see that the wound was healing without a sign of the angry red that would mean infection. When the wound was covered with a clean bandage, she repaired the canoe while he lay and watched.

It was a simple operation. She plastered the duct tape over the damaged area, making a watertight though temporary seal. "I'll repair it properly when we get to Meniskamee," she told him. "But this will do for now."

Michael slept most of that day. His body was healthy and in good condition, and it knew best how to heal itself. So he slept, waking occasionally to watch the patterns the leaves made on the sky as the wind whispered softly through the trees that overlooked the campsite.

132 LAKE OF DREAMS

He woke in the evening feeling much better. His head still hurt, but it was a softer throb now. His muscles felt less cramped and stiff. He even felt hungry. He raised himself on his elbows to a half-sitting position and looked around for Pema. She was nowhere around. Then, from the lake, he heard a splash.

He sat up higher and looked at the water. There was the canoe, but it was bobbing on the water all alone, empty. Where was Pema?

A hand appeared on the far gunwale. Pema's head popped up. She reached across the canoe and pulled herself up until she lay across the canoe. With a lithe twist, she was sitting in the bottom.

But what was she doing? Michael watched in amazement as she walked, bent over and hanging on to the gunwales, until she stood at the bow of the canoe. Turning so that she looked over the canoe, she lifted first one foot then the other onto the gunwales on either side of her. She crouched for a moment, hands still gripping the sides, and Michael could see the canoe rock as she made adjustments. Then, when she was balanced, she slowly stood up.

She stood, tall and straight, water dripping down her body. Her emerald-colored bathing suit glowed, and her skin was golden in the rays of the setting sun. She began to bend her knees and straighten them, jumping without her feet ever leaving the gunwales. Her arms swung, then turned in large circles, adding to her momentum. The canoe bobbed and rocked, up and down, and began to move forward.

Michael watched. His lips stretched into a smile and then opened in a grin. It was funny, in a way, the canoe jerking forward, Pema working away, her long limbs pumping. It was beautiful, too, the slim figure balanced

LAKE OF DREAMS

on the end of the graceful craft, both of them moving together as one. But a gust of wind caught the forward end of the canoe, which was sticking up out of the water, and began to spin the boat.

Pema struggled for balance, her feet adjusting, her arms wavering, and then she was over with a splash. Michael laughed out loud.

She surfaced, shaking the water out of her eyes, and caught the edge of the canoe. The sound of Michael's laughter came to her, and she looked over to the shore. There he was, and not only laughing, he was sitting up! He must be feeling better.

She swam to the bow of the canoe and held on with both hands, swinging her feet up until they were hooked by her heels on the gunwales. She liked gunwale bobbing. It was supposedly a way to propel a canoe if you didn't have a paddle, but was mainly done for fun. It was especially fun when there were two people, at bow and stern, each trying to make the other fall off. Maybe when Michael was healthy again, he'd like to try.

She hung for a moment, letting her head drop back so her hair trailed in the water. The patch on the hull was holding, her canoe was okay, and Michael was feeling better. She dropped her feet into the water and started swimming, towing the canoe, back to shore.

Chapter Seven

Pema ran up the shore to Michael and stood before him breathless and dripping. "Hello, sleepyhead," she said. "You look much better."

"Thank you." He smiled at her lazily. "I feel much better. What a coincidence!"

She felt heat mount to her cheeks as she stood in the warmth of his smile. He looked better than better. The sleeping bag had fallen to drape across his lap, and his bare shoulders and chest looked solid and strong. With his dark hair rumpled from his long sleep, and his face once again filled with color, he looked wonderful. He looked sleepy and satisfied and very sexy.

She dropped her eyes and turned away. "I'll just get changed and then I'll make you something to eat. You must be hungry." She headed for her tent, feeling suddenly shy and awkward. Somehow he seemed like a new Michael, different, but it wasn't he who had changed, she knew. It was she. She knew now that she loved him,

LAKE OF DREAMS

and that changed everything. And it made it impossible for her to stand there and look at him.

Once in a while one of her young boy students at the high school had a crush on her. She knew the look. Sick cow eyes was how she thought of it. All the longing and hope that was reflected in those young faces aimed right at her. It made her feel only pity at the thought of these young men going through all the anguish and power of a first love, a hopeless love, since it was directed at her.

And so how could she stand in front of Michael with his green eyes, which were so alive and observant, and know there was a sick cow look on her own face? For she knew that all that was in her heart must be reflected in her eyes.

She stayed in her tent, drying off and changing into a flannel shirt and jeans, until she felt a little more under control. Tying a turquoise scarf around her neck, she emerged into the last golden light of the sun.

"What would you like to eat?" she asked Michael. She busied herself with the fire, and did not look at him. "Beef Stroganoff or shrimp Creole? Or there's steak, if you prefer."

She could feel his eyes on her and hear him laugh. "Okay," he said. "I'll go along with your joke. I'd like steak, please, and for an appetizer I'll have coquilles St. Jacques. I also want a Caesar salad, and for dessert, well, a chocolate mousse."

She turned to face him, drawn by the warmth of his voice as a moth is drawn to candlelight. She sank to the ground next to where he lay and reached out to touch his cheek. "Oh," she said, "I'm glad to see you so much better. Yesterday, I was afraid..."

He reached up and caught her hand in his. "Pema," he said, and his voice was almost as rough as the beard beneath her fingers, "Pema."

They stayed frozen, neither moving, her hand flat against the side of his face, his hand covering hers. And Pema felt something deep within her open its wings and fly free. Maybe he does care, she thought. Maybe.

It was he who finally broke the spell, drawing her hand to his mouth and kissing the fingers. "So where's this gourmet dinner? I am hungry, and if I don't get my steak soon, I'll have to eat you." He took her fingers into his mouth.

She screamed in mock fear and drew back. Standing up, she said, "I can't provide you with all the food you ordered, but you will eat steak, with a side order of peas. And I can make some 'bout bannock to go with it."

"Steak? Really?" Michael looked around, peering into the trees. "I don't see any cattle here."

"Silly. I always carry a supply of freeze-dried foods with me. And the bannock, well, it's a mix I prepare at home. All I have to do is add a little oil and water."

She dug in the food pack and poured a brownish floury powder into a pot. Adding the oil and water, she kneaded the dough, punched it flat and put it in the frying pan. She put the pan on the grill over the fire until it was good and hot and then propped it on its side, facing the fire, to bake. "There," she said. "You see, it's easy. Woodlands gourmet."

"I'm impressed," said Michael. "But you know, I would really like to get up and wash. I don't want to sound chauvinistic, but maybe while you cook, I can go down to the lake."

LAKE OF DREAMS

"I don't know if you should be up on your feet yet." Pema's forehead creased. "I can give you a sponge bath."

"For heaven's sake, woman, I'm not totally decrepit. I only had a small bump on my head." He pushed the sleeping bag down over his legs. "Could I have some clothes?"

She brought him his jeans and a shirt. He stood up and swayed, feeling dizzy. He was glad of the supporting hand Pema put under his arm. "Okay," he said, "maybe I'm a little decrepit. But if you just help me down to the lake, I'll manage from there."

Pema walked beside him the short distance to the water's edge. He sat on a rock jutting into the water, feeling breathless and still dizzy. His legs were like rubber, and he was glad just to sit for a moment.

"You see," she said. "You're not as strong as you think. We're going to stay here for at least another two days, and you're going to do as little as possible." She put a towel and the other things he'd need on the rock beside him.

"Two days?" He began to protest, but then his head gave a sharp throb and he thought better of it. "Yes, ma'am, anything you say. You're the boss. But I think you're enjoying have me here, so weak, under your thumb."

"You won't fit, either under my thumb or around my little finger." Pema smiled at the truth of this. Even sick and weak, he was so full of power, of masculine energy, that it never occurred to her she could have any sort of control over him.

She left him and returned to the fire to check on her bread. When Michael was done, he called her and she helped him to the fireside. She had brought out the packages of freeze-dried food, and he watched as she ripped the top off one and pulled out what looked like a piece of pressed cardboard. Two pieces of cardboard were put to soak in a pot of water. Another package was full of green confetti, which was poured into a bowl.

"Uh," he said, "I believe in recycling and all that, but isn't eating paper carrying things a bit too far?"

"Paper?" Her voice was innocent, although her eyes were laughing. "Look." She pulled something out of the pot in which the cardboard had been soaking. There was a steak, red and juicy, looking as good as anything Michael had ever bought fresh from a butcher. "And here are the peas," Pema continued, showing him the bowl filled with fat green globes. "I may be an outdoors sort of person, living as naturally as I can, but sometimes I must admit modern technology does have its uses."

Michael lay back against the rolled-up sleeping bags she had arranged as a backrest and watched as she bustled around, cooking the steaks, setting out plates and cutlery, checking the bread. Oh, Pema, he thought, it would be so easy to love you. Here, surrounded by your canoe and the lake and trees, with the setting sun like fire in your hair and the scent of fresh air on your skin. I could hold you in my arms forever. But how could I take you from all this, take you to the city? Even if you agreed to come, if you could overcome your fear, I'm afraid you'd wither so far from all that you love.

The meal was delicious. The scent of the fresh-baked bannock was mingling with the crisp smell of the wood fire as they began to eat. Michael held up a piece of bread that sent soft steam wafting into the air. "What did you call this again?" he asked. "'Bout bannock? I hope I don't regret asking, but why is it called that?"

LAKE OF DREAMS

139

Pema laughed. "You won't regret it, I promise. It's because of the recipe. I use 'bout three cups of flour, 'bout one tablespoon of baking powder, 'bout a double handful of raisins—"

"Okay, I get it." He grinned. "But it is delicious. My compliments to the chef."

She smiled. Michael looked at her, her skin golden in the firelight, and felt himself become lost in the moss green pools of her eyes. Why worry about the future, he thought. With my run through the rapids yesterday, there was a good chance that I wouldn't have any future. We're together now, she and I, here in this magic world.

He reached out and caught the end of her scarf in his hand. "It's nice of you to always wear a handle," he said. And he pulled her closer to him until his lips could reach hers.

Pema let her plate slide to the ground. She lay on her front beside him, propped on her elbows. His hand was still firmly wrapped around her scarf, and she could feel the material tight on the back of her neck, but it didn't matter. Nothing mattered except the feel of his mouth on hers, his lips moving, his tongue teasing. She was lost in a soft, moist world so that when he let go of the scarf and drew his lips from hers, she swayed forward and fell onto his chest.

"You taste like steak," he said.

"How romantic."

"Well, it's better than if I'd said you taste like pressed cardboard, which was what I was sure you were going to feed me."

She laughed and sat up, looking for her plate. She felt dizzy, and her limbs were so weak that she had to concentrate very hard to coordinate her fingers to pick up

140 LAKE OF DREAMS

the plate. Boy, she thought, it took a blow on the head and a tumble through the rapids to disable Michael. All it took for me was one kiss.

She firmly marshaled her thoughts and stood up. "I must do the dishes. It was smart of you, to get yourself hit on the head so you could get out of doing all the work."

"Good planning, eh?" He lay back against the sleeping bags, realizing that he was very tired. He yawned. "I've had a hard day. It's tough, you know, sleeping all day."

"I can imagine." Pema filled a plastic tub with hot water and washed the dishes. When she was done, she sat by Michael and they both stared into the dying embers of the fire.

"My brothers will be worried," she said. "I always radio them from the cabin when I go to the lake. But they won't be too worried. They know my travel time can vary, depending on weather and other conditions."

"You go often to the lake?" Michael found a stick and poked it into the fire, sending showers of sparks into the darkening sky.

"As often as I can." She fell silent, remembering that this trip was probably her last one.

"Will it hurt you badly, losing Meniskamee?"

Pema stared at him, wondering if he had read her thoughts. "Yes," she said simply, "it will."

A silence fell. The end of Michael's stick caught fire and he held it out, watching the tiny flames licking at the wood. He brought it to his lips and blew, extinguishing the flames. A gray coil of smoke rose from the stick's tip.

"Why?" he said finally. "I know you told me about the memories the place holds for you, your grandfather and so on, but surely a part of the joy of canoeing and

LAKE OF DREAMS 141

traveling through this land must be seeing new sights. Couldn't you get just as much pleasure from exploring new lakes, from making new terrain part of you?''

Pema watched the stick Michael was again poking in the fire. ''Why do you ask? Why do you care? You're going to take Meniskamee from me, no matter what I say.''

Beside her she heard him draw in a breath and expel it into the darkening night. ''Yes,'' he said. ''I am. It sounds like the place I've been looking for, and your family needs the money.''

She stiffened, the motion drawing her away from him, but his hand closed over hers.

''I'm sorry,'' he said. ''I don't want to hurt you. But we must move forward, you and I. I need the retreat for my company. And you, you must move on to what life holds for you instead of clinging to the past.''

Pema felt like screaming. How could he talk like this to her? Who did he think he was, a wise old father? And what did he know about past and future, especially hers?

''You do see what I mean?'' he asked gently.

''I don't know what I see. And how can I try to explain what the lake means to me? You'd never understand.''

In the firelight, Michael saw a glint on her cheek. A tear. ''Try me,'' he said softly.

''Meniskamee is me.'' Pema was sitting up straight, her clenched hands resting on her bent knees. ''It's the place where I learned who I am. I was a person there, I was myself. And Grandfather was there, is there. He showed me my world and taught me I could be part of it. At Meniskamee I fit in, I was accepted. I wasn't just the little girl of the family, I wasn't a person set in a mold. I was free.''

142   LAKE OF DREAMS

She was crying in earnest, and her words were choked out between sobs. "And it still is true. When I go there, I am free, I am Pema."

Michael pulled her rigid body against his wide chest. "Pema, oh, Pema, you're a person no matter where you are. You don't need a special place in which to be yourself, you carry who you are wherever you go. You're a special person, an individual who has a lot to offer, to other people and to the environment you care so much about. But who you are is in you, not in a pool of water surrounded by cliff and trees."

He held her, his words flowing soothingly around her ears. He stroked her hair, her back. He rubbed the back of her neck, until at last her sobs quieted and her stiff muscles relaxed.

"You can get by without your lake," he said. "I know I sound hypocritical. You probably think that since I want to take it away from you it's in my best interests to convince you, but I really believe what I'm saying. You can do anything you want, you can achieve your dreams, and you don't need a special place, only yourself."

Pema said nothing. She lay against him, her cheek on the wet spot her crying had made on his shirt. She wanted to believe him, she wanted so much, but she was afraid. What sort of person am I, she wondered, to have dreams, but never the courage to try? A new thought entered her mind. I am, it said, the sort of person that Michael can say this sort of thing to. I am the sort of person he believes in. This thought was so new that she quickly banished it to the back of her mind, to be brought out and examined more closely some other time. But she felt the weight on her chest lighten, and she sat up and smiled at him.

LAKE OF DREAMS

"That's my girl," Michael said. He kept his arm around her shoulders and pulled her to lie beside him, leaning on the sleeping bags. They sat beside the glowing embers of the fire and watched as, one by one, the stars filled the sky.

"I think," he said, after a time, "I'd better get to bed. I'm falling asleep right here, and it's nice, but I think I'd be more comfortable inside my sleeping bag."

Pema slipped reluctantly from under his arm and stood up. "Sleep is what you need. I'll just lay out your bag inside your tent." She left him sitting by the fire while she carried the two bags they had been using as a backrest over to the tents. She crawled into his tent and spread his bag out. On her knees beside it, smoothing out wrinkles, she thought back to the past night when they had lain together, the two of them cocooned within this nylon bag. Legs entwined, arms wrapped around one another, sharing warmth, they had slept and it had been right. But it wouldn't happen tonight.

Last night he'd needed her, her body heat and her physical presence, at least, and she'd been glad to provide them. But tonight he was himself again, though still weak and sore, and he didn't need those physical offerings. She wondered if he would ask her to stay. But she unrolled her bag within the green walls of her own tent.

He didn't ask. Michael was half asleep already, stumbling as she helped him into his tent. She laid him on his bag and tugged his jeans off. He was asleep before she had zipped him up.

She knelt for a moment in the mouth of the tent, watching him in his sleep. The planes of his face were softer, but the growing blackness of his beard gave him a piratical look even in sleep. He looked peaceful, though, and happy. She crept up to his side and kissed his cheek. His eyelashes, so long and dark, made half circles on his cheek, and looked so lovely that she kissed his eyes and his nose, too. Then she went to her tent and prepared for bed.

The next two days passed amid golden sunshine, gently lapping water and laughter. Michael was up early the second day of his enforced inactivity. The sun wasn't even up yet, but he felt refreshed and stronger.

Pema was awake, too, and when she heard him stirring she called to him to come out and see the morning.

The air was very still. The grass was damp with dew, and the surface of the lake was still. Already, though, the warmth of the coming sun was drawing wisps of mist up from the land and the water. Pema and Michael sat side by side on the shore, the lake lapping at their feet, and watched the sun rise.

It was worth watching. A smudge appeared on the horizon, a simple lightening of the night sky at first, but the gray soon began to blush red. The color spread, tingeing the few clouds in the sky with pink and then orange. Streaks extended across the water toward the two watchers, orange sparkling with gold. And still the colors grew, washing across the sky, brightening and changing until, almost with a fanfare, the edge of the sun appeared.

Michael let out his breath. "Glorious," he said. "Do you know, I've never watched a sunrise before."

Pema turned questioning eyes to him. "I've seen sunsets, of course," he continued, "and I've seen some sunrises on mornings when I was just coming home from a very late night, but I've never just sat and watched a sunrise."

LAKE OF DREAMS 145

"It's hard to get up early enough," she said. "Just before dawn is the time when a warm bed is most appealing. But I've always felt it was worth it, the times I have gotten up to watch."

"Bed gravity. That's what it is when your bed is so comfortable and your limbs are so heavy that the thought of getting up seems impossible. A bed is one of the most powerful sources of gravity known to modern science."

"Bed gravity!" She laughed.

The air was still silent with the early morning calm, but a few birds had begun to try out their first calls of the day. Pema and Michael felt too comfortable sitting by the lake to move. "Shore gravity," he said. They sat in companionable silence, broken once in a while by Pema, who was trying to identify for Michael the birds they heard.

And then from out on the lake, a gibbering, high-pitched cry was heard. Michael's fingers tightened on Pema's. "What is that?" he asked.

"A loon. Wait—yes, there he is. Look."

He looked at the lake and saw a bird shape floating about twenty yards out. It rode lower in the water than a duck, and he could see a white band around the dark-feathered neck. The bird suddenly disappeared beneath the surface of the water.

"Where did it go?" He scanned the water. "Did it sink?"

"Wait." Pema moved her eyes, searching the area around where the loon had disappeared. "There he is." The small head popped up out of the water, joined by another. "They swim, almost like flying, under the water. They're looking for their breakfasts. Speaking of which, do you want yours?"

146   LAKE OF DREAMS

Michael nodded, his attention still on the loons. The eerie cry came to him again. It spoke to him of the loneliness of the vast, empty reaches of this wilderness. And yet he didn't feel alone. He felt he was part of it.

Pema drained the last of her coffee and sighed with satisfaction. "Nothing like coffee," she said, "even if it is drunk three hours after you've woken up. Come on, let's go for a canoe ride."

"What?" Michael looked up from where he was leaning against the rolled-up sleeping bags. "I thought I was supposed to take it easy."

"Don't worry, you will." Pema put the canoe into the water and helped Michael to sit in the bottom, leaning against the stern seat facing the bow. She arranged a life jacket as a cushion for him. "There. Comfortable?" She sat in the bow, facing him, and pushed off.

"Hey, this is rather nice." He leaned back, trailing one hand in the water.

She laughed. "All you need is a parasol and you'll look like one of those Victorian ladies, you know, the ones who were rowed along the river by their swains."

"You don't look like a swain. Where are we going?"

"Oh, I don't know. Let's go exploring. I want to know what's around that point of land there."

The canoe moved smoothly through the water. Michael tilted his head back, feeling the rays of the sun warm on his face. He was feeling better. The pain in his head was almost gone, as long as he didn't make any sudden moves. The sound of the water lapping at the canoe was soothing; the feel of the water beneath was like a gentle hand holding him.

They rounded the point and found a marshy area along a tree-lined shore. Tall weeds grew out of the wa-

LAKE OF DREAMS

ter, green and fleshy, with sharp edges to their long leaves. Michael looked over the edge of the canoe. The bottom of the lake was mucky, but he could see the weeds growing out of the mud, and other smaller plants that hadn't yet made it up to the air and sunshine. There was a sudden swirl of silt in the clear water.

"Hey," he said. "I saw a fish."

"Good," said Pema. "I was hoping to find a place like this. And I just happened to bring along my fishing rod." She paddled the canoe to a position just outside the weeds and pulled her rod case from under the thwarts. "Here, you can handle the landing net. But make sure you don't move too fast, and keep your weight in the center."

"I'm not sure I want to keep my weight anywhere other than where it is." Michael looked at the net suspiciously, wrinkling his nose as if he expected it to smell fishy.

"Don't tell me, you've never been fishing, right?"

"Well, no, I haven't. I don't like to kill things."

"Oh, listen to this," Pema jeered. "You were certainly happy enough to eat the fish I killed the other day."

"True. They were delicious. But listen to us. We sound like we've switched roles. I thought you were the environmentalist. Don't all life-forms have equal rights?"

Pema selected a lure and sent it flying across the water, making sure her back cast went behind her, over the bow of the canoe and nowhere near Michael. "Yes, I believe that. But I never said that resources shouldn't be used at all. It's common sense. Take only what you need, and do it in such a way that you disrupt the environment as little as possible. And make sure you don't take more than can be naturally renewed."

148 LAKE OF DREAMS

Michael thought that this could have the makings of a good argument, but he felt too good to bother. He lay back, listening to the splash of the lure and the whirring of Pema's reel. The canoe gave a lurch. He sat up and saw Pema struggling with a bowed rod and a taut line.

She had a fish. Michael wasn't sure if he was glad or not. Fresh fish for supper would be nice, but he didn't really want to deal with a flopping, half-dead fish at close range. Cleaning the fish she had caught earlier on the trip had been bad enough.

Pema reeled in her line and held up a dark, wriggling form. "A pike," she said. "Bony. But we'll keep it anyway. I have a feeling that's all we'll catch here." She seemed to recognize Michael's hesitation, took the net from him and landed the fish herself. He looked at the fish, lying still in the bottom of the canoe, then settled himself back with a sigh.

The canoe drifted slowly before the wind. Pema picked up her paddle once in a while and moved them into areas she was sure were exactly where the fish were waiting. She caught two more pike. "Oh, well," she said, "we'll head back now, and troll on our way."

She had better luck with this technique, catching one walleye and one lake trout. She was smiling as she beached the canoe and ran to get her bucket and filet knife. Michael eyed the knife warily.

"Don't worry," she said. "I won't ask you to do the dirty work this time. I only asked you the last time because I wanted to see the fastidious city man up to his elbows in fish guts."

Michael sat down, well out of range of the silver scales flashing through the air. "I knew why you asked me. You thought I wouldn't do it, you thought I'd be grossed out."

LAKE OF DREAMS

"I admired you," she admitted. "You did it, even though it was obviously distasteful to you, and you did a good job, too. But you know what my main reason for getting you to do it was? I really hate cleaning fish!"

He laughed. "Here, do you have an extra knife? I'll help."

"It's okay. You're convalescing. If you feel up to it, though, you can get the lunch things out. We'll have peanut butter on the leftover bannock, and I think there's cheese left. And some dried fruit."

After lunch, Michael had a nap, lying under the trees, drifting off to the sound of the wind whispering in the leaves. Pema felt energetic, despite the early start to her day, and wandered off into the woods, searching for edible plants. Michael awoke to find her shredding unfamiliar-looking leaves into a pot.

"What are you doing?" he asked.

"Making a salad for our supper."

He looked at the piles of strange-looking plants on the ground beside her and wondered if he was still asleep and having a nightmare. "Whatever happened to good old lettuce and tomatoes? And cucumbers?"

"Those things don't grow out here, in case you hadn't noticed." Pema began slicing a thick white root. "Anyone who spends time in the bush should learn how to find food. It's always possible you'll spend more time traveling than expected, or you may lose your supplies. A little plant lore can mean the difference between survival and starvation. And besides, these things are good. Here, try this." She held out a purplish green leaf.

He nibbled on it tentatively. It wasn't bad, a little bitter, perhaps, but it tasted fresh and crunchy.

"Amaranth," she said. "It grows in cities, too, as a weed. Probably even in Toronto. Just think how impressed your friends will be the next time you give a dinner party, if you serve a weed salad."

Michael thought about the people he had over to dinner in his home in Toronto. Business associates. Women he dated. He liked cooking, actually. He often cooked a meal rather than taking a woman out to dinner. They seemed to appreciate the effort, as long as the meal was good. But those people would not be impressed by weed salad.

The salad—which they ate with the fresh fish and a new loaf of bannock—was good. Pema had made a dressing for it, using lemon juice and spices. She seemed to have a never-ending array of small amounts of various cooking ingredients, all kept in tiny waterproof containers.

"Do you know," said Michael, as they sat digesting and watching the shadows of the trees lengthen across the water of the lake, "I've never spent a day like this before. A day doing nothing."

"Nothing," said Pema indignantly. "You watched the sunrise, and went fishing, and ate weed salad, and—"

"I know. But understand, to me a day like this would always have been considered wasted. I didn't get any work done, nor did I do anything physical, you know, work out. In the past, even when I was sick, I had paperwork brought to the house, so I could still get things done. I was always busy, working, partying, seeing shows, meeting people. It never occurred to me I could spend a day like this. And you know what? I wasn't bored today. Not once."

He looked so pleased with himself that Pema swallowed the retort she was about to make about the impossibility of fishing from a canoe in downtown Toronto.

LAKE OF DREAMS 151

"You know," he continued, "when I was growing up, there were always people around who said that during life you should take time to sniff the daisies. I begin to see what they meant."

"Tell me about Toronto," Pema said.

She sat beside him, nestled into his side, his arm warm across her shoulders, and listened as he made the city come alive for her. He spoke of picnics on Centre Island, of cultural events, plays and art shows at Harbourfront, of walking down Yonge Street at night just to look at the people. He told her about street musicians, classical groups as well as guitarists, playing under the bright neon lights, and people strolling, buying chestnuts or hot dogs from street vendors.

"There are so many stores, you can find anything you want, and many things you never knew you wanted. And the libraries, so big, you can spend a lifetime learning. And museums. You'd like the museums, Pema. I don't go to them very much, but I like knowing they're there. But you'd go, you'd love having so many worlds to explore."

Pema spoke in turn, telling Michael about Saskatoon. "It isn't a small town, it's a city, though not nearly the size of Toronto. But because we're so far away from the big centers, we're very self-sufficient. There's a lot of culture, plays, music, art. There's the river, with parks running along both sides, and people cross-country ski there in the winter, and walk and jog and bicycle in the summer. And friendly. People who visit from the east always comment on how friendly and open we are."

The sky darkened and the stars came out, and still they talked. They were open to each other. They wandered together through worlds new and familiar. They drank deeply of one another's souls. The voice at the

152 LAKE OF DREAMS

back of Michael's mind that told him this was wrong was still there, though. I can't get this close to her, he thought. It will only hurt her more when I buy her lake and then return to Toronto.

But the voice was quieter now, muted by a day spent in the joy of her company. He reached for her, pulling her into his arms, and sought her lips with his. And he ignored the voice as it asked, You think of her pain when you leave. But what of yours?

The next day was another that rippled and flowed and sang. They didn't watch the sunrise because they'd gone to sleep very late, but they did go fishing. This time Michael took the rod and learned about lures and casting. And when he caught a small pike, his grin was just as wide as that of any fisherman who catches the big one he's always dreamed of.

He paddled the canoe for a short time, pleased to feel the strength returning to his muscles. His head felt fine, and the bandage had been taken off. In the heat of the afternoon they went for a swim, and the cool water removed the last stale feelings from Michael's body.

"I am ready to go on," he announced.

Pema smiled at him, happy to see him so restored. She, too, was ready to go on, for Meniskamee was calling her, but she was sorry that these golden days were ending. And she was afraid, too, of what would happen when Michael saw her lake and wanted it.

They spent one last night at their campsite, for Pema wanted to be sure Michael was rested and fit enough. Early the next morning, while the sun's rays slanted between the leaves of the trees, they loaded the canoe and were off.

"Say goodbye to the Laughing Spirit," said Pema.

LAKE OF DREAMS 153

"The spirit nearly had the last laugh," said Michael. He'd wandered along the shore of the rapids earlier that morning, while Pema took down the tents. He'd stood on a rock overlooking the chute guarded by the two boulders and had stared into the water foaming and roaring its way down the stony drop, dodging and twisting between the scattered rocks.

And now, as they paddled away across the sun-dappled lake, he did not look back.

Chapter Eight

"It's not much farther now," Pema said. The canoe was almost all the way across Clarendon Lake, approaching Desiree River.

She was feeling the breathless anticipation she always felt when she neared her lake. Desiree was the gateway, the passage into enchantment.

Michael, in the bow, was also glad that the trip was drawing to an end. Although he felt totally recovered from his mishap, he still tired more easily than he would have liked. And he was pleased to think that his long search was at last coming to an end. He wanted to see this lake that he had heard so much about. He knew it would be perfect, exactly what he needed for his company's retreat.

He was curious, too, to see if Meniskamee was really as special as Pema seemed to think. Was it different from other lakes, so that it, and only it, could mean so much

LAKE OF DREAMS 155

to her? Memories could imbue a place with lifelike qualities, but still . . . For a moment, Michael almost expected that they would see her grandfather, standing on the shore in front of the cabin, waiting to greet them as they arrived.

He shook his head, dispelling the silly image. Meniskamee was a lake like any other, maybe a little prettier, but still a lake. And it was the lake he had traveled so far to buy.

Another image came to his mind, of Pema in the moonlight, her face streaked with silver tears as she tried to explain to him why Meniskamee was special. She had wanted so badly for him to understand. Why? So that he could share that important part of her, so he could see a little deeper into her soul? Or so he wouldn't take the lake away from her? Michael didn't want to think about it. He plunged his paddle into the water, his back straight, and pulled hard, each stroke drawing the canoe a little closer to Meniskamee.

Desiree River was magical. They left the wide expanse of water that was Clarendon Lake and passed between overhanging trees on the shore. Michael hadn't even seen the mouth of the river there, and had thought that Pema was taking the canoe in to shore. But a narrow passageway opened up before them and they floated beneath the trees, the leaves reaching down to trail over their faces.

The bright glare of the sun faded, leaving only a cool, green-and-silver light. Sounds became hushed, as if even the birds and insects recognized this was a special place. They floated along the river, their paddle strokes slow and even.

The river was narrow and shallow. The trees that grew along each bank held their branches out, some dipping into the cool water, others extending across to meet with their fellows on the opposite shore. The effect was that of a tunnel, a round green-and-brown passage with walls and ceiling of living, whispering leaves. The air was cooler here, and very sweet. Birdcalls from among the trees were sharp and clear.

Michael was entranced. He stopped paddling, absorbed by the beauty that lay all around him. What a special world. How good it would be for his employees, how it would refresh their minds and prepare them for the seminars and presentations that awaited them at the lake. He knew now, with certainty, that he had been right to decide that ideas would best flow in natural surroundings. The clear air and water of this place would clear minds, too, cleansing all whom he brought here of the clutter and dirt of the city.

He shook his head and resumed paddling. He was being silly. His staff would probably never see this river. He couldn't bring them all in by canoe, and this river was too narrow and shallow for a motorboat. The young men and women would have to be flown in. Oh, well, if the lake was anywhere near as special as was this river, the benefits it offered would be just fine.

He'd make canoes available, though. Maybe a course in learning to handle a canoe would be a standard part of the retreats.

He laughed soundlessly at himself. He'd come a long way on this trip, and not just in terms of kilometers traveled. If anyone had suggested last week that time spent paddling frail little boats could be beneficial to the functioning of his company, he'd have thought they were crazy.

The river meandered through the forest, twisting lazily through the trees. Pema knew every bend, every

LAKE OF DREAMS

turn. There, that was the sandbank on which she had once seen a moose. That had been a special moment, the animal standing tall, his proud rack of antlers seeming impossibly big. He had stood still for a moment, raising his head to look at her as she drifted past, the water dripping from his muzzle. Then he turned, with great dignity, and vanished into the forest.

That grassy bank there was where she usually liked to stop and sit for a while, holding off for a few minutes her arrival at Meniskamee. Coming to the lake was so special she liked to savor it, and she would sit on the grass all alone and feel herself opening and expanding, becoming ready to enter the world she truly belonged in.

Today, however, she paddled the canoe past the grassy bank. She wanted to hurry on. She was both anticipating and dreading the moment when the canoe would pass out of the river and onto the waters of the lake. Anticipating because of her love for the place, and dreading because of Michael. It would be his first look ever at Meniskamee. What would he think? She wanted him to love it as she did, to understand. But if he loved it he would buy it, and it would be lost to her. So she paddled on, driving the canoe silently through the water, each paddle stroke both too fast and too slow.

The river began to widen and the trees grew straighter, allowing the sun and sky to come down between their branches. The water moved a little faster, gurgling and chuckling, for here it was fresh from its source. They passed between the last guarding trees, and the lake opened up before them.

It was small and very deep. Cliffs lined the northern shore, and there was a sandy beach across from them. A little way up from the beach, on a grassy knoll, stood a cabin. Its wooden walls blended in to the forest that

158 LAKE OF DREAMS

stood behind. The edges of the lake, as they circled from beach to cliff, were ragged, fingers of water poking in between trees, forming little bays and coves. It was beautiful.

By unspoken agreement, Pema and Michael lifted their paddles and rested them across the gunwales. The canoe drifted and bobbed on the sparkling waters.

Pema's heart was full. But a faint, unfamiliar thought niggled at the back of her mind. Yes, I am here, and it is very lovely and it holds many precious memories, but it is only a lake. Maybe I am ready to move on. She quickly banished the idea from her mind. She was tense, obviously, at the thought that this was probably her last time here.

Michael sat up on his seat and gazed with wonder at the lake. What a place! It far surpassed all his hopes for the site of his retreat. So isolated, so lovely, so peaceful, it was perfect. The cabin was too small, of course. Other buildings would have to be erected. He felt a moment's regret at the thought of other structures cluttering the pristine shore. The cabin built by Pema's grandfather blended in so well with its surroundings, it seemed almost to add rather than detract from the natural beauty. But a good architect could be brought in to design buildings that would fit in as well.

He'd obviously have to restrict the number of people who could come here at one time. And he would have careful rules to make sure they didn't mess up the environment. He wouldn't want this lovely lake polluted, its shores cluttered with garbage. No, he would be careful, he would be a good master of this land.

Pema's voice seemed to enter his mind, flowing softly as if whispered. No one can be master of this land. If you were master, the land would cease to be what it is.

LAKE OF DREAMS

159

It is what it is because it is free and proud. Only by accepting it as it is, by becoming part of it yourself, can you hope to dwell here and share in all it has to offer.

Behind him, he heard Pema pick up her paddle. He took his, too, and together they brought the canoe to the sandy beach. Pema sprang to the land and ran to the cabin. She opened the door and disappeared inside. The door, Michael noticed, had not been locked.

Pema stopped in the main room of the cabin, her arms outstretched, and whirled her body around. It felt so good to be here! She explored the familiar surroundings, the two tiny bedrooms, the large room that served as kitchen, dining and living room. The wood she had left laid in the fireplace the last time she had been here was still there. The cupboards contained the stock of canned and dried foods that had been flown in by the last plane to come here, earlier in the spring. It was home, all was here waiting for her.

Michael came in, carrying the packs. She smiled at him, her joy at being here so great that she could forgive him for being here himself.

"Well?" she demanded. "Do you understand now? Can you see that Meniskamee is special?"

He grinned at her. Her eyes were so bright and clear, her cheeks flushed with excitement, her hair flying behind her as she dashed from place to place. "Yes," he said. "I see it now."

She stopped suddenly in midstride as she dashed to the linen closet to air bedding. "Oh, I must call my brothers."

The radio sat on a small table in a corner by the kitchen. Michael watched as she fiddled with dials. Then the far-off voice of her brother Peter was heard.

160 LAKE OF DREAMS

"Hello? Pema, is that you? What happened, honey, that you took so long? We were a little worried."

"Nothing to worry about," she said into the microphone. "Everything is fine. We had a little holdup on the way, that's all." She briefly described Michael's accident.

"He's hurt?" Peter's voice was louder now. From behind him, Pema could hear the voices of her other brothers, asking questions, sounding alarmed. "He should be seen by a doctor."

"Peter, that isn't necessary. He's fine, really he is."

Michael stepped up and took the microphone from Pema. "Hello, Peter? Oh, it's John. Listen, I appreciate your concern, but I really am fine. No, it was nothing, just a small bump on my head. No, I don't need to come back." He listened for a minute. "I see, well, yes, I understand, but I don't think it's necessary. But thank you."

Michael returned the handset to Pema. "Now I see where you get your stubbornness from," he muttered as she took his place at the radio.

"Don't you worry about a thing, sweetheart," she heard John say. "We'll take care of everything." And he cut off the connection before she even had a chance to open her mouth to protest.

Michael smiled. "It's nice to have someone worry about me, even though I know they're mainly concerned that I injured myself so badly that I'll hate this whole province and won't buy the lake."

"You're awfully cynical," Pema said indignantly. "They care about you. They're worried that you may be really hurt. And after all, blows to the head are something you have to be very careful about. For all we know, you could have damaged something in your brain."

LAKE OF DREAMS 161

"Don't worry, no one could tell the difference, even if I did." Michael went out to the canoe to bring in the last of the gear.

They finished unloading and had lunch. Pema didn't eat much. Why were her brothers so overprotective? Had she really grown up with that? She started washing the dishes.

Michael dried the last plate. "Hey," he said, "don't look so sad." He drew his finger down her nose. "I'm fine, you know. We're here, where you wanted to be. Let's go for a swim.

"Okay." She dug her bathing suit out of the pack and went into one of the bedrooms to change. Michael was right, everything was fine. Why did she feel so full of unease and tension? Even if he was going to buy the lake and this was her last time here, she should be happy and enjoy the lake while she could. And maybe he would say it was okay if she came here once in a while, whenever there wasn't a retreat going on.

She searched his face as she came out, longing to learn from his eyes whether or not he was going to buy the lake. He had said he understood why it was special. He loved it, too. But did he love it because of what it was, a beautiful piece of natural environment, or because it was the place he wanted for his retreat? She was afraid to ask. She would ask, she had to know, but not just yet. Maybe there was a chance he wouldn't buy it. She would swim and hope while she could.

Michael took her hand in his as they ran down the bank and onto the sandy beach. They plunged into the water, sending a silvery splash into the air. Michael lifted her in his arms then leaped forward, sinking chest first into the water. Pema clung to him, closing her eyes as she felt the cool water rise over their heads. He stood, still holding her against him. He was laughing, and he shook his head, sending drops flying from his hair.

She felt her face open in a grin. How could she possibly be in a bad mood when Michael was like this, so happy, so fun, so lovable? She squirmed to be free, and got one foot on the ground. Michael gave a mock growl and tightened his grip, but she wriggled free, laughing, and was running through the water toward the beach. She heard him splashing behind her, and his hand reached out and snared her wrist. He came up behind her and snaked his foot around her ankle as she ran, and she was falling, then she was lying on her back in the sand with Michael on top of her. The shallow water ran over their bodies, little waves that sent ripples over her skin, as he took her mouth with his.

He kissed her until all thoughts of the lake and her family's money troubles were long gone from her mind. Her senses were filled, but only with sand and water and sky and the feel of Michael, hard and solid, covering her. His mouth was warm and moist, and he tasted of the freshness of the air and the water.

A wave bigger than most came rushing up and surged over their faces. They sat up, sputtering and laughing. Pema's hair was full of sand. She took the hand Michael offered to help her stand up and ran out to deeper water to rinse her head. And then she started swimming with long, hard strokes across the lake to the cliffs.

Michael followed her, keeping up easily with the pace she set. They reached the base of the cliffs.

Pema treaded water, putting out a hand to feel the gray granite wall. "The lake is deep here. These walls go straight down for about thirty feet. They're riddled with caves."

LAKE OF DREAMS 163

"I want to see a cave." Michael flipped over onto his back and floated, staring up at the trees leaning over the top of the cliff.

"Okay, follow me." He heard her take in a breath of air, and then there was a splash, but when he lifted his head to see, she was nowhere in sight. "Pema," he called, "where'd you go? Show me the cave. Or did the big wave from the other lake sneak in here and grab you?"

He heard laughter, muffled but unmistakably hers, coming from the solid wall. There was a flurry of water near his feet and he looked down to see her lithe form, green-and-silver through the water, swimming to him.

Her head popped above the surface. "Come on, there's a sort of tunnel underwater. It's not long, though. Follow me."

Michael filled his lungs with air and ducked under the water. His powerful arms pulled him smoothly through the green depths, following Pema to a dark opening in the cliff wall. A couple more strokes and he was through. He came to the surface, took a breath and looked around.

He was in a round room, totally surrounded by stone. The water was deep, and the walls rose quite high, their surface covered with ledges. There was a light source somewhere above his head and he looked to find it.

"There's an opening there to the outside," Pema said. "Bushes grow on the outer wall of the stone there, so you can't see the hole from the lake, but if you climb that ledge there, you can see out. This was my secret cave when I was a kid. I brought all my treasures here, and spent hours playing. All those little shelves there—" she pointed "—were filled with all my special things. And there's even a seat over here.'' She moved to one of the walls and faced him.

There was a ledge a couple of feet under the surface, which made a perfect place to sit. Michael maneuvered his body to it and sat. The water came up to the middle of his chest.

"When I was a kid, I couldn't sit here very well.'' Pema's eyes were never still, moving around the ledges, seeing the treasures that were long gone. "Even when I was tall enough, I was too light. As soon as I got my bottom onto the bench, I kept floating up. So I had what I thought was a very smart idea. I got a piece of rope, and I tied two rocks, one on each end, and then I used it like a weight belt. With it across my lap, I could sit here as long as I wanted.''

"Isn't that a little dangerous, though?'' Michael asked. "What if you'd become tangled in it? The water's pretty deep in here.''

"That's what Grandfather thought.'' Her laugh was rueful. "Boy, was he ever mad when he heard about it. I'd gone to him, all excited about how clever I was, and he really let me have it. He told me that even though I was a child of the water, I still had to be sensible. The waters would take me if they had the chance, so I must always treat them with careful respect. And weighting myself down with stones was not respectful. The water gave me buoyancy as a gift.'' She gripped the edge of the stone bench with her hands and let her feet float up in front of her face. "I was a bit smart-alecky, and I asked why the water would give me the gift of the ledge that was a perfect bench if it didn't want me to sit on it. Well, Grandfather's face went even darker, and he said that the water was not providing my little bottom with a seat, the ledge was simply part of the living stone. It was self-

LAKE OF DREAMS 165

ish to see parts of the environment only in how they related to me. I started to cry then, I remember, I was so afraid Grandfather would make me leave the lake, and I was also afraid he'd give me something for my bottom himself, and that it wouldn't be a bench.''

''So what happened?''

Pema wriggled her toes, enjoying the feel of the cool water between them. ''He hugged me and told me that he loved me. He told me I was very young, and I would learn. And then he came out here with me, and we found a rough knob of stone, and we fastened a short rope to it so that I could hold on whenever I sat here, and keep myself from floating away.'' She dropped her feet and twisted, feeling along the rock wall with her hand. ''Here's the knob, right here, but the rope is long gone.''

Michael groped with his hand and came upon the softness of hers, the fingers curled around a protrusion of rock. His fingers closed on hers, and he felt a breathlessness as her hand turned in his, her fingers entwining with his.

''You have me floating,'' he whispered.

''That's not hard, considering you're chest deep in water.'' But her eyes were smiling.

He reached for her and she drew near, and he lifted her until she sat on his lap. They stared at each other, eyes wide with wonder. Slowly, Michael reached out, tracing his finger along her brow, down her nose, over her high cheekbones. And then he kissed her.

His mouth roamed over her face, nibbling her chin, sliding across her cheek, licking the tip of her nose. Pema giggled and stopped his wandering lips with her own. Her lips parted; her tongue reached for his.

Now that his mouth was at last concentrating on one place, Michael's hands began to roam. They slid up her

166 LAKE OF DREAMS

arms, cupping her shoulders, and then caressed her neck. He felt the smoothness of her back, the hard lines of her ribs, and then his hands moved around to the softness in front.

Pema heard a moan start low down in Michael's throat as he cupped his hands over her breasts. The moan was echoed within her, for his fingers had slipped beneath the material of her bathing suit and found the sensitive nub of her nipple.

Michael pulled the straps of her suit down over her shoulders. She made no protest, moving her arms to free them of the material. The water was cool on her bare skin, but it did nothing to quench the fires she felt within.

He lifted her up, holding her half-floating before him as he buried his face between her breasts. He kissed the hollow between them, and turned so his face was pressed against her softness.

"I remember this," he whispered. "When I was coming back after my accident, I came out of the blackness and found myself in a world of pink softness." He circled her nipple with his tongue, and Pema shivered, arching her back so that she was pressed harder against his face.

His hands were moving again, up and down her back, cupping her buttocks, pulling her hips so that she was pressed against him and could feel the hot, hard urgency he felt for her. His fingers traced little circles on her stomach, and his mouth took hers again. The circles were growing bigger, each one covering more skin, each one moving lower until his finger brushed the material of the bathing suit, rolled down to her hips.

He cupped her hipbone in his hand, and then his finger was slipping down the crease made by her thigh,

LAKE OF DREAMS 167

slipping slowly toward the core of the fire that consumed her.

Her ears were filled with a roaring and a throbbing. She leaned back, allowing his hand easy access to the place no man's hand had yet touched. She was filled with need, she ached with it, she yearned, and she did not yet know what it was she needed to fill her emptiness.

But slowly an awareness was working its way through the gold haze that filled her mind. The throbbing she heard was more than the beating of her heart, the roaring was louder than the sound of her blood rushing through her body. She lifted her head.

"Michael! There's a plane out there."

He looked up, too, his eyes heavy-lidded and glazed. "What?"

"A plane. A plane is coming in for a landing on the lake."

They looked at each other in the half light within the cave. Then Michael buried his face in her neck with a groan. "Do you think that maybe they'll just think we're not here, and go away?"

"Oh, we can't do that. They can see there's a canoe here." Pema's whisper was full of regretful longing. "It may be someone who needs help."

Michael gently set her down on the stone bench and climbed up ledges until he could see out the opening. "You're right, I can see it, a small float plane circling for a landing."

Pema was pulling up her bathing suit. She felt dazed, her mind sluggish, her limbs slow to respond. She could still feel the caresses Michael had covered her body with, could still feel the heat of his mouth branding her breasts. She followed him as he dove under the water and went out through the tunnel.

168 LAKE OF DREAMS

The plane landed just as they reached the sandy beach in front of the cabin. Pema looked out as it coasted to a stop before them. The door opened, and her brother John climbed onto the pontoon.

"Hi, Michael," he called. "It's okay now, your long ordeal is over. We've come to rescue you."

Pema and Michael looked at each other, surprise and dismay in their eyes. Then they burst out laughing.

All their protestations were useless. John had come out here, chartering a plane away from the forest fires by telling the pilot about the emergency. He was determined to take Michael to a doctor.

"A head injury is a serious thing," he said. "You can't fool around with your brain. And besides we, my brothers and I, feel responsible. After all, we did sort of get you out here under false pretenses. You expected to be flown to the lake, not canoed."

Pema stood frozen, staring at her brother without seeing him. Her body was still heavy and warm, she could still feel the imprints of Michael's hands and mouth. She knew what they had been moving toward, she and he, knew what would have happened if they hadn't been interrupted. She had wanted it so!

And now, when it was important to concentrate on what was happening, her mind wouldn't function. But surely Michael wouldn't leave. "I'm glad I had the chance to travel by canoe," she heard him say.

Her mind cleared suddenly and she turned on John. "See, you heard him. He feels fine and he's glad he traveled by canoe. This hasn't been an ordeal." She faced Michael, expecting to see warmth and a hint of laughter in his green eyes as he shared this joke of her

LAKE OF DREAMS

brother's overreaction. But what she saw sent a sudden chill through her heart.

Michael wasn't looking at her. He stared across the lake, his gaze seemingly focused on the rock wall that hid her treasure cave from view. She had a feeling that he wasn't thinking fond thoughts of what had so nearly come to pass in the half darkness behind the cliff.

"I am fine." Michael turned to John. "I appreciate your concern. But since you've gone to all this trouble because of me, I think I will take advantage of the plane being here. I've seen all of Meniskamee I need to. I'll return to Saskatoon with you."

Pema's mouth fell open. "What? You haven't seen anything. You haven't seen the beaver dam, or the spot where I saw a bear. You haven't been on top of the cliffs." She felt the shock cut through her, but was unable to ask the real question. What about me? What about us?

"Excuse us a moment," Michael said to John. He took Pema's arm and walked her along the beach and into the shadow of the forest that crowded the lakeshore.

"I have seen enough," he said. "I wish I could share the other places that are so special to you, but it's better for your sake if I don't."

Pema was suddenly conscious of her wet bathing suit and hair. She wrapped her arms around herself for warmth. "What do you mean?"

Michael gently rubbed his hands up and down her arms. "You're very beautiful," he said. "Especially here in this setting. What almost happened between us in your cave, well, I wanted it very much. But I'm glad that it didn't happen."

170 LAKE OF DREAMS

She heard herself whimper, a small sound high in her throat. She stepped back, away from the heat of his hands. The trees surrounding her, usually so welcoming, seemed to close in around her, dark and menacing.

"Don't you see?" he asked. "We have no future, you and I. You belong here, in the sun and water. My place is in the city with the smog and crowds. I thought at first, I thought maybe..." His words trailed off and his eyes locked with hers. His gaze was so warm, so tender, that Pema felt tears start in her eyes. She blinked them back.

He leaned forward and kissed her on her trembling mouth. "You have to find your own way," he said, so softly that as he turned and walked away from her, she wondered if she had truly heard the words.

It took no time at all for Michael to load his things into the plane. He took one last look around the shore. Pema, standing by the edge of the trees, couldn't tell if his gaze included her or not.

And then he and John were in the plane and it was skimming along the surface of the lake. She watched as it took off, as light and graceful as a dragonfly. She stood perfectly still, staring into the sky, until the plane dwindled and disappeared into nothingness.

Chapter Nine

Pema walked through the forest, her feet following a path that, although faint, was well known to her. Last autumn's leaves covered the ground, brown and dry, their veins all that held the brittle things together.

She walked slowly, her head down, watching the dead leaves crumble beneath her feet. It seemed to her that the path was never ending, that it moved beneath her so that no matter how many steps she took, no matter how hard her legs pushed against the ground, she got nowhere. It was all the same, this trail, hard-packed dirt covered with a loose mulch of dead vegetation.

Still, the path took her, as she had known it would, around the lake, ending on top of the cliffs on the north shore. She sat on an outcrop of stone high above the waters of the lake and rested her chin in her hand.

Her eyes sought out the patch of sky where she had last seen the plane, and she shook her head and dragged her gaze away with a snort of annoyance. What good did

172 LAKE OF DREAMS

it do to look there? Did she think he would return to her, that he would order the pilot to turn back? But why had he gone and left her with this emptiness inside?

She told herself that the emptiness was because of questions unanswered. She didn't know if he was planning to buy her lake. He hadn't said anything that would even give her a hint. How could she stand not knowing? How could she stay here not knowing if it was the last time she would swim these waters, walk these trails? Was she to be left with nothing? No lake and no Michael.

No Michael. She had only just begun to appreciate all that being with him meant, and now he was gone. Was he right in believing that their relationship held no future? Had his growing affection for her—and she did believe that he felt something—been nothing more than closeness born of opportunity? If so, he was right to have done what he did, for she knew how much greater the pain would be if he'd left her after they'd become lovers. It had been nothing more than a shipboard romance, she thought, her lips twisting wryly. A canoe-board romance.

You must find your own way, he'd told her. Her way, alone, without him.

While she sat and thought, the lake began its healing magic. The wind blew softly over the tops of the cliffs, whispering through the tall grasses and wisping through her long, loose hair. A chickadee landed on a bush near where she sat, looking at her with its bright dark eye before calling in its metallic voice, "Chick-a-dee-dee-dee!"

She looked up. The chickadee bobbed on its little legs and called again. She felt herself smile. The bird, with its little black cap, looked so cocky, so pleased with itself. I am here and it is wonderful, it seemed to say.

LAKE OF DREAMS 173

She felt the sun warm on her back, and saw how, with the fading of the light, the colors of the world around her were taking on new depths. Greens were brighter; the grays of the stone were richer. A blue jay streaked across her line of vision, its wings a blue so deep it made the sky pale.

She took a deep breath, filling her lungs with the air that smelled of earth and water. She felt a new source of strength, of life even, a source that didn't come from this land she loved so well. It came from within herself.

Pema spent the next few days alone at the lake. She repaired her canoe, using fiberglass matte wetted with resin to build up the broken area. When she was done she looked critically at the repaired area. It showed, the scar would always show, but the area was as watertight and strong as it had ever been. The canoe was ready again to take on any water she might care to venture into.

She spent a lot of time swimming and walking. She covered all the trails through the forest paths over which she had once run lightly as a child. She saw how the summer's leaves were growing full and green on the branches of the trees, replacing those she crumbled underfoot. In places along the path, new growth was pushing its way toward the sun. Countless baby trees, their life dropped onto the rich soil by the tall giants, were putting out their first leaves on spindly little branches. Most of them, Pema knew, would not survive the summer. They wouldn't get enough water, or sun, or air. They'd be beaten down by wind or rain. But some of them would make it, to grow a little taller and a little stronger the next year. And all of them were trying, all of them were hoping, as they put out their fuzzy light green leaves and searched for the sun.

174   LAKE OF DREAMS

Pema went swimming every day. One day she decided she was going to swim all the way around the lake. This was no mean feat. Even without all the bays and coves, the shore of the lake was at least two miles in circumference, the distance she'd tried to cover only a couple of weeks ago. But she knew she had to try.

She felt good as she set out, her body limber, her muscles strong. Her feet kicked, her arms pulled, flashing in the sun as they were lifted, one at a time, swinging forward over her head to plunge into the water ahead.

By the time she neared the cliffs on the opposite shore, she was beginning to tire. Her breath was ragged, and it was more of an effort to lift her head far enough to the side to take in a breath of air. A wave slapped her in the face, and she took in a mouthful of water. She treaded water for a minute, waiting until she stopped coughing.

She had come a little more than halfway around. There was no shore to rest upon here if she needed it, only sheer cliff walls rising overhead. But she didn't need to stop. She was tired, but she could still go on. She needed to tap her inner reserves of strength and learn how deep they were.

She swam on, switching to breast stroke. She left the cliffs behind, rounding the eastern shore, swimming through shallows in which water lilies grew. She was approaching the last stretch. She could see the sandy beach coming closer, each stroke moving her through the water and nearer to her objective.

She knew she could do it. This swim would not turn out like the other one had. She knew now that what she had been trying to prove then, to Michael and to herself, was rooted in her insecurity. She had been trying to force a strength into being that didn't exist. But this time she could sense the strength, deep within herself. It was there, an inner confidence. The strength was there to help her carry out whatever task she set herself. And so now, even though she was tiring, she never doubted that she could do it

She walked up the shore, water streaming from her body. She felt a little shaky, her legs were trembling and she was cold, but inside she felt a sense of power and heat. She had done it. She had tried and she had succeeded.

It was time to leave. She knew she was ready. She stood on the cliff top for one final time.

"Goodbye," she whispered into the wind. "Goodbye. I thank you for all you have given me. And goodbye, Grandfather. You were always there for me when I needed you. You have helped make me what I am. But I'm grown now. I must set out on my own and leave behind all that has supported me before. I must try."

The wind ran past her, carrying her words to the trees and the birds. She stood tall, at the very edge of the cliff, poised between sky and water.

The canoe moved toward the shore of Meniskamee where Desiree River began. Pema left the lake, slipping into the silver green waters of the river. The canoe floated easily, surging ahead with the stream, for now she was moving with the current instead of against it. And as the canoe left Meniskamee and disappeared behind some trees, she did not look back.

Pema pulled her car into the gravel driveway in front of her brothers' farmhouse. She'd called ahead to let them know she had returned, and now they poured out

176 LAKE OF DREAMS

the kitchen door to envelop her in the warmth of their hugs.

They were all speaking at once, telling her of goings-on at the farm during her absence and asking how her trip had been. Then she heard the name she'd heard echoing in her mind ever since she watched a float plane dwindle against the bright sky.

"Michael left," Peter was saying. "He wouldn't go to the doctor's appointment we'd set up."

"We were surprised," John added, leading the way into the house. "We thought it a bit odd that he would leave without getting in touch with us. For one thing it was rude, after we'd rescued him and all, not to let us know how he was."

"But most of all," said Peter, "we were surprised because he never let us know whether or not he was buying the lake. He did like it, didn't he?"

Pema collapsed onto the bench at the table with a sigh. "Oh, yes, he liked it. Very much."

"Good." John rubbed his hands together. "And how do you feel?"

"You do see, honey," Peter said, "how important this is to all of us, to the farm. With the money from the sale, we'll be able to go on."

Four pairs of eyes stared anxiously at her.

"I have no objections," she said. "If Michael Christie wants to buy Meniskamee, he has my blessing."

Her brothers began to clap and cheer, and she was enveloped in a fresh round of hugs. When she had extricated herself from the last rib-crunching display of affection, she stood up and spoke again.

"I'm going away, you see. I'm going to the University of Toronto, to start graduate work in biology."

LAKE OF DREAMS 177

Her brothers fell silent, their whoops and cries of joy falling from their lips.

"What?" said John. "You, go to that city, all alone? Who'd look after you?"

"Pema," Peter was saying at the same time, "how can you go so far, away from all your family and friends? You won't know a soul."

Even the twins spoke up, voicing their dismay.

"I am an adult," Pema said. "I love you all very much, and I know you love me, but in your love you still see me as the dependent little sister you petted and took care of. I've grown up. I have something to offer to the natural world I love so much, and the only way to do that is to go back to school and get a higher degree. I have to try. I'm ready to try."

She left her brothers standing there, the four of them in a row, protests dying on their lips, and returned to her car to unload the canoe.

The arrangements were easy. She phoned Professor Hathaway in Toronto. He was delighted to hear she was finally coming. She explained that she would no longer be able to carry out her original proposed research, the ecological study of Meniskamee Lake.

"No matter," he said. "There are lots of valuable projects for you to do right here."

She called the high school to tell them she wouldn't be returning to her job. She sublet her apartment. She stored her things at the farm, packing only those small things she wished to bring with her to her new life. No, not her new life. The continuation of her life.

Her brothers all came to the airport to see her off. "Please," she said, "if Michael Christie ever calls, do not tell him where I am. I don't want him to know my

178 LAKE OF DREAMS

address or my phone number. I don't even want him to know I'm in Toronto.''

Pema loved Michael, and always would, but it was like her love for her lake. She was grateful to Meniskamee, for giving her the strength and knowledge she needed to be going after her dream. Michael, too, had helped her take this first step, and she was grateful to him. But like the lake, he was gone. He was no longer part of her life.

The apartment Professor Hathaway had found for Pema was perfect. It was in a part of Toronto called Kensington Market, and the neighborhood was filled with people and stores from all over the world. In the early morning she would wake to the sounds of awnings being rolled open and voices calling to one another in Spanish and in Chinese. She had two rooms on the second floor of an old building that housed a bakery on the ground floor, and every morning her bedroom would be filled with the scent of fresh-baked bread.

Her neighbors were friendly and curious, and she soon felt on easy terms with them. Other students lived there, as well as the families that ran the stores, and she spent evenings sitting on the floor of tiny apartments, discussing world events and university happenings, drinking red wine and eating cheese and crackers.

She wandered the streets of the city and explored. Just as Michael had predicted, she loved the museums, and spent many hours gazing at dinosaur bones in the Royal Ontario Museum or pushing buttons in the Ontario Science Centre.

But it was her work with Professor Hathaway that gave her the most satisfaction. He put her to work at first in the lab, so she could learn how to use the equipment. He soon had her out in the field, though, collecting samples for a study he was doing.

LAKE OF DREAMS

She spent her time along the shores of Lake Ontario, and on the outlying Toronto islands, doing research into how the polluted lake was affecting the bird populations. She was using her life to give something back to the environment, and her work was totally fulfilling.

Her fears of the competition the other students represented were completely unfounded. The people she worked with weren't out to get her. They were her colleagues. For the first time, Pema could talk about her feelings about the natural world with people who understood. She was amazed at how quickly she settled into the life of university and city.

Frequent thoughts of Michael, though, made her aware that the hollowness that had been with her ever since they had been interrupted in her treasure cave was still there. Unlike Meniskamee, he had not faded to a warm memory with only an occasional ache of loss. The pain of Michael's leaving was still sharp and strong.

She looked him up in the phone book, half expecting that he'd have an unlisted number, but he was there. His address burned itself into her brain. One day she set out on a streetcar that would take her to the street where he lived.

Michael had not, as yet, done anything to finalize his purchase of Meniskamee, and he could not have said why. He'd returned to his company and reported that his trip had been successful, that he'd found the perfect site for the retreat. The money for the purchase had been authorized, and he'd said he'd handle the transaction himself. But that had been weeks ago, and still he'd done nothing.

He tried not to think about why he was doing nothing. For if he did, his mind was filled with an image, an

180 LAKE OF DREAMS

image of a woman with long red hair and moss green eyes. His ears would fill with the song of her voice, and he would breathe in and smell her scent that was a blend of wood smoke and the perfume of flowers. He didn't want to think about her. She wasn't here with him. And that hurt.

He threw himself into his work, putting in longer days and bringing paperwork home. He plunged into the summer social scene, going to parties, meeting people at clubs, escorting beautiful women to plays and concerts. It didn't work.

It did fill the time, and it kept him busy, but it didn't banish the images from his mind. Pema was there, singing her songs, swimming through sparkling lakes, dancing along forest trails. He wanted her.

The women he dated seemed superficial and shallow. Before, he'd always prided himself on the fact that he dated prominent models and actresses, the most beautiful women in the city, but now their heavily made-up faces seemed artificial, like masks that hid the emptiness behind their eyes. Their talk was boring, full of petty intrigue and gossip, and their favorite topic of conversation was always themselves.

His work, too, no longer held the same fascination it once had. He found himself wondering if it really mattered how many computers were sold, or if yet another word-processing software package was developed. It didn't matter to him. He began to wonder why he worked so hard. His work paid well, true, but it left him with no time to enjoy anything. He was surprised at these thoughts. He'd always thought that he did enjoy life to its fullest. But now his old pursuits were empty and he longed for something fresh and natural in his life. He longed for Pema.

LAKE OF DREAMS   181

She wasn't here. Michael did up the pearl buttons on his silk shirt and glanced at his watch. His date was waiting for him downstairs. She was someone new, a model he hadn't taken out before, but he had a feeling that this evening would be indistinguishable from countless others. Still, it was better than spending the evening alone. If he was alone he'd begin to think, and then he'd rush to his office to find work to fill up his emptiness.

He hurried downstairs and bustled the woman out the front door to where his car was parked. They were late for the theater and so he jumped quickly into the driver's seat without seeing the woman with long red hair who stood on the sidewalk just down the street.

Pema had felt foolish as she approached Michael's house, but still something drove her on. There it was, a lovely house, made of red brick with many gables and balconies. Just the sort of house she liked. She paused a little way down the street, in the shadow of a tall tree. Then the front door opened and Michael came out.

He looked so good, dressed in a dark suit with pants that clung to his lean hips and a jacket that emphasized the breadth of his shoulders. Pema opened her mouth to call. She could feel the song mounting in her heart. But then she saw that he wasn't alone.

He escorted the woman, holding her elbow, and opened the car door for her. The woman was very elegant, terribly thin, but she held herself with great dignity. Her hair was pale blond and it was sticking out all over her head in one of the new styles. She wore a fur coat, even though the evening was warm, but it was open in front to reveal her white, sequin-studded dress.

182   LAKE OF DREAMS

Pema didn't wait to watch the car drive away, but returned to the streetcar stop, her feet leaden. That was it, then. If that was the sort of woman Michael liked, well, he couldn't possibly have ever seen anything in her. But she wouldn't let this get her down. She had inner strength, she knew it now. She'd been tested in other ways and she'd come through. She would come through this, too.

Michael returned home early. He had brought the date to a close as soon as he could after the final curtain fell, realizing that he couldn't take another night of useless conversation and too much to drink. The model had been surprised, and a little insulted, when he dropped her off and didn't ask to come inside her apartment. He had shaken her hand and thanked her, and walked away.

And so now here it was, only eleven o'clock, and he was home alone. He wasn't ready for sleep yet, so he headed for his study and opened the top file on his desk. It contained the report he had filled out describing Meniskamee.

All right, the time had come, he would do something about that darned lake. He would buy it. Right now. Saskatchewan was in a different time zone, it was earlier there. He picked up the phone.

Pema's brother Peter answered. He was delighted to hear from Michael, and even happier to hear that Michael was definitely interested in the lake.

"We had wondered," Peter said. "But we didn't like to bother you, and we thought maybe you were still convalescing from your terrible accident."

Accident was right, thought Michael. But it had been his heart, and not his head, that carried the long-term scars.

LAKE OF DREAMS

183

John came on the line. "We've had papers drawn up, just in case. They're all ready to send to you, except for one thing. We need Pema's signature."

Michael felt impatient suddenly. He wanted to get off the phone. "Well, get it and send me the papers. I can take care of everything if you send me the name of your lawyer."

"There's a problem." John's voice was hesitant. "Pema isn't here."

Michael sat up straight, alarm in his voice. "She's okay, isn't she?" He had a sudden vision of her having an accident while she was paddling home, alone with no one to help her.

"She's fine," said John.

Michael could hear, in the background behind John, the voices of his brothers. There seemed to be some sort of argument going on.

"Tell him," someone said.

"But she didn't want anyone to know. Especially not him." John's voice was muffled, as if he had his palm over the receiver, but Michael could still hear.

"Tell him," the other voice said. "He can easily get her signature. We need the money now, and it's silly to send her the papers and have her send them back and then us send them to him."

"We promised," John said firmly, and then he was back on the phone. "It will take a few days to reach Pema, but we'll get her signature. No problem."

Michael heard no more. Slowly his hand lowered the receiver to its cradle. If it was easy for him to get her signature, it could only mean one thing. Pema was here, in Toronto. And she hadn't wanted him to know.

A rush of thoughts ran through his mind. She had done it, she had overcome her fear and had gone after her dream. He felt a burst of pride fill his heart. She was here, at the university. But she hadn't wanted him to know. She didn't want to see him. She was here in the same city, but she didn't want to even speak to him.

Michael sat in the study for a long time. Then he opened a new file folder and began to scribble some notes to himself. He would follow his own advice. He would find his own way to go after his dream.

Pema had filled up the evening working in the lab. Now it was late, but as she reached home she heard the phone ringing through her closed apartment door. She fumbled with her key and burst into the room, grabbing the phone. It was her brother John. Michael had called. He was buying the lake. John would send her some papers and she was to sign them and return them to him. Pema, her whole body numb, agreed without really listening. The lake was already gone, had been sold long ago in her mind. She would sign anything. And Michael was gone, too.

The next morning she returned from the library and decided to stop at the bakery to get a cinnamon bun to have with her lunch. The sound of voices floated out the open door of the store. Pema smiled. Frank, the baker, was engaged in one of the heated but harmless arguments he loved so much.

"How can you say that?" his deep voice was demanding. "The government knows nothing. How can a bunch of men in three-piece suits who have lived here all their lives know anything about what it's like to come to Canada on a boat, tossed around in a dark hold? Canada means nothing to those politicians compared to what it means to a refugee who sees it as a golden land of stability."

LAKE OF DREAMS

185

"Hey," said another voice, laughing. "I agree with you. Canada is an important symbol to those people. But we need a system that works to insure that people who are genuine refugees are taken in ahead of others who want only economic opportunities."

Pema froze. The second voice was familiar to her also. It was a voice she still heard in her dreams. She stepped through the bakery door, and there was Michael. He was leaning on the counter, one hand holding one of Frank's special honey wafers, the ones he never sold, but baked to give to special friends. Michael's hair was different, combed straight without a sign of the curls she'd twined her fingers through. And his face, too, what was it? Oh, she knew. During the last days they'd spent together, his beard had been growing, emphasizing the lean line of his jaw, shadowing his cheekbones. But now, without the stubble, the firm line of his lips was cleaner and his dimple suddenly flashed into view. The two men were grinning at one another, plainly enjoying their discussion.

Frank looked up and saw Pema. "Ah, here she is. This is the one you were waiting for, no? And well worth waiting for, I say!"

"Yes," said Michael. He turned to face her, his green eyes searching her face. "Well worth it."

"He came looking for you," said Frank, his wide apron-clad form bustling around the counter. "I found him standing in the street. Can't have that, I thought, so I brought him in here. Smart man, he is, but a little mixed up about the government. I'm trying to set him straight, but I can see it'll be a hard struggle."

"I'm a slow learner," said Michael grinning. "But once I learn something, I never forget." He turned to Pema. "May I come in?"

186   LAKE OF DREAMS

She went to the stairs that led to her apartment. She was speechless. Michael was here. He was going to be in her apartment. They would be together, he and she. But why? Why was he here? Did he have the papers she was supposed to sign?

She opened the door and led the way in. Michael stopped a few steps in and looked around. He was in a small foyer, which led into a living room. She had decorated the rooms in forest greens and browns. It was a lovely room, serene and natural, a perfect setting for Pema.

She stood facing him. She wore black jeans and a rust-colored sweater made out of a soft clinging wool. A brown scarf shot through with gold threads hung loosely around her neck. Her green pools of eyes were full of questions and fears. And hope. When Michael saw that, he dropped the large envelope he was holding and held out his arms to her. The envelope fell to the floor unnoticed as they came together.

Pema walked forward until his arms enfolded her and drew her against him. His chest was warm and broad and firm, and she felt as though she had returned from a long journey as she felt her body mold against his. And when his lips found hers, she let her head fall back, her long hair falling over his hands, and she closed her eyes and lost herself in him.

When after a long while they drew apart, they stood grinning at one another. Then they both spoke at once.

"How did you—" Pema said.

"I came to bring you—" Michael said.

They both laughed. She took his hand and led him to her sofa. "You go first," she said.

LAKE OF DREAMS 187

He picked up the envelope he had brought with him and sat next to her. "I have some papers for you to sign." He handed the envelope to her.

She looked at him, a question in her eyes, and opened the envelope. In it were papers that stated that Meniskamee Lake, in the Province of Saskatchewan, was to become the sole property of Pema Robinson.

She raised her head, her eyes wide. "But you're buying Meniskamee."

"I am," said Michael. "But I know the lake belongs to you. I am transferring ownership to you. I was hoping we could come to some sort of agreement. Maybe I could rent it from you and hold retreats there while you're here in Toronto. But I can find another place if you prefer. Meniskamee is yours, to do with as you wish."

"I don't understand." Pema looked at the papers in her hand. "You were so sure you wanted it."

"I want it all right. But there's something I want more." He took one of her hands in his. "I was wrong, thinking we had no future. I thought I was right and so I didn't give you a chance. Didn't give us a chance. But I couldn't get you out of my mind. And when I learned you were here— Well, I'm so proud of you, darling." He lifted her hand to his lips and kissed her palm. "I had a dream. You had a dream, too, and when I learned that you had gone after your dream, and were making it come true, I thought that maybe there was hope for my dream, too." He leaned toward her, his breath warm on her cheek, and wriggled his tongue into her ear.

Pema giggled for his tongue was tickling her even as it sent fiery waves through her body.

188 LAKE OF DREAMS

"What is your dream?" she asked. Her breath was a little jerky, for Michael was now tracing a path of little kisses along her cheekbone.

"My dream," he whispered, "was that we could share the lake. My dream—" and now he was nibbling the tip of her nose "—was that we could share our lives."

"Share?" she asked, her words whispered against the soft warmth of his neck.

He pulled his head back the minimum distance necessary to look into her eyes. "Share," he said firmly. "Our lives together. I want you to marry me. We can live in Toronto while you need to be here for classes. When you can get away, or want to do research, we'll go to the lake."

"Will we travel by canoe?" she asked innocently.

"All the way to Saskatchewan from Ontario?" His voice was surprised, but then he must have seen the smile she knew was escaping through her eyes. "Pema, darling, I'd paddle across Canada with you if that's what you want."

She allowed her smile to reach her lips and felt it spread inside her until her heart was smiling, too. She tried to pull him closer but he held back, clearly wanting to say more.

"After your degree," he said, "well, this is something I've been thinking about for a while. I want to leave my company. We can travel, go wherever you can use your skills. And perhaps we can work together, my knowledge of computers enhancing your work with the environment."

"Leave your company?"

He nodded. "It runs smoothly without me. I have good people working there. It might even run better without me."

LAKE OF DREAMS

She laughed. "You're too good at delegating. And too efficient."

"You're not too efficient. You still haven't given me an answer. Will you marry me?"

Pema wrapped her arms around him, one hand sliding into his hair. "I don't know," she said. "Your hair isn't curly. How do I know you are the Michael I love?"

"Because I am the Michael who loves you. We are each a half, Pema, separate halves, but together we make a whole. And if you wish . . ." He sat up and ran the fingers of both hands through his hair, rumpling it until it curled in wild disarray. "If you wish, I'll never comb my hair again."

"It doesn't matter," said Pema. She looked into the sparkling green of his eyes. "As long as we're together, nothing matters." And she parted her lips to receive his kiss.

* * * * * *

NORA ROBERTS

Love has a language all its own, and for centuries, flowers have symbolized love's finest expression. Discover the language of flowers—and love—in this romantic collection of 48 favorite books by bestselling author Nora Roberts.

Starting in February 1992, two titles will be available each month at your favorite retail outlet.

In February, look for:

Irish Thoroughbred, Volume #1
The Law Is A Lady, Volume #2

Collect all 48 titles and become fluent in the Language of Love.

LOL192

THE LANGUAGE of LOVE

Take 4 bestselling love stories FREE

Plus get a FREE surprise gift!

Special Limited-time Offer

Mail to Silhouette Reader Service™

In the U.S.	In Canada
3010 Walden Avenue	P.O. Box 609
P.O. Box 1867	Fort Erie, Ontario
Buffalo, N.Y. 14269-1867	L2A 5X3

YES! Please send me 4 free Silhouette Romance® novels and my free surprise gift. Then send me 6 brand-new novels every month, which I will receive months before they appear in bookstores. Bill me at the low price of $2.25* each—a savings of 34¢ apiece off cover prices. There are no shipping, handling or other hidden costs. I understand that accepting the books and gift places me under no obligation ever to buy any books. I can always return a shipment and cancel at any time. Even if I never buy another book from Silhouette, the 4 free books and the surprise gift are mine to keep forever.

*Offer slightly different in Canada—$2.25 per book plus 69¢ per shipment for delivery. Canadian residents add applicable federal and provincial sales tax. Sales tax applicable in N.Y.

215 BPA ADL9   315 BPA ADMN

Name _____ (PLEASE PRINT) _____

Address _____ Apt. No. _____

City _____ State/Prov. _____ Zip/Postal Code _____

This offer is limited to one order per household and not valid to present Silhouette Romance® subscribers. Terms and prices are subject to change.

SROM-91   © 1990 Harlequin Enterprises Limited

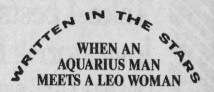

WHEN AN AQUARIUS MAN MEETS A LEO WOMAN

Unpredictable Aquarian Alex Sinclair liked his life as it was. He had his horses, his work and his freedom. So how come he couldn't—wouldn't—leave fiery veterinarian Katrina Rancanelli alone? The love-shy widow obviously wanted no part of him, but Alex was determined to hear her purr.... Lydia Lee's THE KAT'S MEOW is coming from Silhouette Romance this February—it's WRITTEN IN THE STARS.

Available in February at your favorite retail outlet, or order your copy now by sending your name, address, zip or postal code, along with a check or money order for $2.59 (please do not send cash), plus 75¢ postage and handling ($1.00 in Canada), payable to Silhouette Reader Service to:

In the U.S.
3010 Walden Avenue
P.O. Box 1396
Buffalo, NY 14269-1396

In Canada
P.O. Box 609
Fort Erie, Ontario
L2A 5X3

Please specify book title with your order.
Canadian residents add applicable federal and provincial taxes.

SR292